Tradin' Paint

Raceway Rookies and Royalty

Tradin' Paint

Paint

Raceway Rookies and Royalty

by Terry Bisson

SCHOLASTIC INC.
New York Toronto London Auckland Sydney
Mexico City New Delhi Hong Kong Buenos Aires

PHOTO CREDITS

p. 6 (Richard Petty): Duomo; p. 10 (Lee Petty): AP Photo; p. 17 (Kyle Petty): Duomo; p. 20 (Bobby Allison): AP Photo; p. 24 (Donnie Allison): AP Photo; p. 26 (Davey Allison): Lynne Sladky / AP Photo; p. 30 (Michael Waltrip): Tony Gutierrez / AP Photo; p. 34 (Darrell Waltrip): Mark Humphrey / AP Photo; p. 40 (Dale Jarrett): Chris Trotman / Duomo; p. 45 (Terry Labonte): Mark Humphrey / AP Photo; p. 50 (Bobby Labonte): Terry Renna / AP Photo; p. 52 (Dale Earnhardt): Chris Trotman / Duomo; p. 60 (Dale Earnhardt Jr.): Chris Trotman / Duomo; p. 63 (Jeff Gordon): Chris Trotman / Duomo; p. 72 (Mark Martin): Chuck Burton / AP Photo; p. 77 (Ward Burton): Chuck Burton / AP Photo; p. 81 (Jeff Burton): Matt York / AP Photo; p. 83 (Jeremy Mayfield): Bob Brodbeck / AP Photo; p. 89 (Tony Stewart): Nick Wass / AP Photo; p. 95 (Steve Park): Chuck Burton / AP Photo; p. 100 (Kevin Harvick): Ric Feld / AP Photo; p. 108 (Matt Kenseth): Pat Crowe II / AP Photo; p. 112 (Kurt Busch): Mark J. Terrill / AP Photo; p. 116 (Greg Biffle): Donna McWilliam / AP Photo.

PHOTO CREDITS: INSERT SECTION

I (top): AP Photo; I (bottom): AP Photo / HO, Petty Enterprises; II: AP Photo; III (top): JS / AP Photo; III (bottom): David Graham / AP Photo; IV (top): Chris O'Meara / AP Photo; IV (bottom): Chris Trotman / Duomo; V (top): Chris Gardner / AP Photo; V (bottom): Grant Halverson / AP Photo; VI (top): Wade Payne / AP Photo; VI (bottom): Tony Gutierrez / AP Photo; VII: Mark J. Terrill / AP Photo; VIII: Terry Renna / AP Photo; IX (top): Chuck Burton / AP Photo; IX (bottom): Tim Sharp / AP Photo; X (top): Chris Trotman / Duomo; X (bottom): Chris Trotman / Duomo; XI (top): Pat Crowe II / AP Photo; XI (bottom): Grant Halverson / AP Photo; XII (top): Chuck Zoeller / AP Photo; XII (bottom): Chris Trotman / Duomo; XIII (top): Chris Trotman / Duomo; XIII (bottom): Tom Ryder / AP Photo; XIV: Alan Marler / AP Photo; XV (top): Eric Gay / AP Photo; XV (bottom): Chris Trotman / Duomo; XVI: Nick Wass / AP Photo.

ISBN 0-439-34127-2

12 11 10 9 8 7 6 5 4 3   1 2 3 4 5 6/0

Printed in the U.S.A.   40

First Scholastic printing, December 2001

For my car-crazy son,
Nathaniel

Table of Contents

Introduction

Stock car racing has come a long way in a little over fifty years — from a bunch of speed-crazy country boys with souped-up cars to America's fastest growing spectator sport.

The first drivers were bootleggers showing off the fast cars they used to outrun the police. This outlaw pastime soon grew into a sport, which spawned a circuit of short tracks (under a mile), most of them located in the South.

The tracks were dirt, when the weather was good; mud or dust, when it wasn't. Sometimes at Daytona the cars slid off the sand into the ocean surf!

NASCAR (National Association of Stock Car Auto Racing) was formed in 1947 to standardize the rules and keep the promoters honest. A big crowd at an early NASCAR race would be five thousand fans. Prizes were in the hundreds of dollars.

In the 1950s, the cars were truly "stock" — just like the ones you could buy off a dealer's showroom floor. There were Hudsons, Kaisers, and Studebakers (all extinct today, like the dinosaurs), as well as Chevies, Dodges, Pontiacs, and Fords.

Horsepower was increased with high-compression

Tradin' Paint

heads and extra carburetors. Wedges were put in the springs to improve cornering. Seat belts and a roll bar (sometimes made of wood) might be added for safety. But that was about it.

"The cars were still pretty stock when I stopped racing in 1956," NASCAR great Herb Thomas remembers. "They had everything in them. Glove box, cigarette lighter, radio. You could listen to the radio during a race!"

Often a driver worked on his own car. Then he untaped the headlights, changed the tires, and drove it home after a race, hoping he wouldn't get a ticket for his loud exhaust!

Racing was a "guy thing." Most of the drivers were hard-charging "beat-and-bang" racers, each with a football helmet, a chaw of tobacco, and a lead foot. They didn't attract big sponsors because they weren't always great role models.

That was then.

Today's racetrack is paved with asphalt and seats hundreds of thousands of fans, while millions more watch on television. Half the fans are women. Prizes are in the millions of dollars.

Today's race car bears no resemblance to the Ford or Pontiac your mom or dad might buy at the dealer. It is a 700-hp steel-and-fiberglass pure-speed machine that has spoilers to keep it on the ground. It is built by a team of fabricators, engineers, and mechanics in an air-conditioned shop, then hauled to the track in a half-million-dollar trailer along with a ton and a half of spare parts, tools, and even extra engines.

The drivers themselves often fly in private jets and helicopters. Their sponsors range from McDonald's to Home Depot and include many of the biggest corporations in the world.

And yet . . .

In some ways stock car racing hasn't really changed at all.

It's still about fast cars.

It still requires skill, daring, teamwork, and luck.

It's still about the smell of burning rubber, the roar of the crowd, the scream of thirty to forty unmuffled engines, and the powerful adrenaline rush of wide-open competition.

It's still lots of fun for the drivers, their crews, and the fans.

It's still one of the most exciting sports in the world!

Auto racing in the USA ranges from go-karts, with tiny wheels and lawnmower engines, all the way up to the 200 mph bullet-shaped Indy cars (often called "open wheelers" because they have no fenders) that compete at the Indianapolis 500 every year.

Stock cars are the most popular because they look like the cars you see on the highway. Underneath they are as high-tech (and as fast) as Indy cars, and may cost even more. But the "sheet metal," the body, must copy a Pontiac, Ford, Dodge, or Chevy.

NASCAR sponsors three national series. The Winston Cup is the big one, with the fastest cars and the biggest prizes. The Busch Series is for cars that are only slightly lighter and less powerful. The Craftsman

Tradin' Paint

Truck Series is for pickup trucks with 700-hp engines. Many drivers work their way up, starting in the Craftsman Truck Series, advancing to the Busch Series, then arriving at the Winston Cup. NASCAR also sponsors several regional series for "Late Model" (stock body), "Modified" (minus the fenders), and "Featherlite" (less than full size) stock cars.

In every NASCAR series, drivers (and owners) race for points, which are awarded for finishing the race and for leading laps, as well as for winning. For example, in Winston Cup racing, the winner of a race gets 175 points, while the leader of each lap gets five. (In theory, this means that the last place driver could get more points than the winner. One way this could happen would be if a driver led a 300 lap race for 200 laps, then came in last.) The driver who has accumulated the most points at the end of the season wins the championship.

Though NASCAR is the biggest auto racing organization, it's not the only game in town. Indy cars, sports cars, and drag racers all have their own organizations, with their own rules and regulations. Sprint cars (1500 pound open-wheelers) are popular on short tracks. And for beginners (especially kids aged five to fifteen), there are fiberglass-bodied 150-cc quarter midgets. As you will see in this book, many NASCAR superstars started out driving go-karts, quarter midgets — or even BMX bikes!

This book is about drivers.
Stock car drivers are celebrities. Racing fans root

4

for their favorite drivers, wear their colors, collect their autographs.

"The fans identify with us," Darrell Waltrip once said, "because we drive cars. Everybody drives cars!"

But the drivers themselves will be the first to tell you that they are only one part of a team. It takes a small army of skilled and dedicated people to put a stock car on the track, much less at the head of the pack.

So remember as you read this book that behind every driver there is a team that includes crew chief, engine builder, pit crew, and dozens of others, all burning with the desire to win.

And that's what makes racing — teamwork!

This book is for fans.

"Without the fans," Richard Petty once said, "I'm not Richard Petty."

Racing fans are special. They do more than just cheer. They know what their favorite drivers are up against. They know the cars, the other teams, and the other drivers. They know the tracks. Racing fans are very knowledgeable. That's why what you are doing now, reading and learning about the sport, is so important.

So before they say "Start your engines!" you know what to do —

Open your books!

The Petty Family

Richard Petty started third at the Daytona 500 in 1991, but dropped back early on in the race.

Richard Petty was stock car racing's first superstar. He won seven Winston Cup championships, seven Daytona 500s, and more individual races (two hundred) than any other driver before or since.

He won pole position — the best spot on the track, reserved for the fastest driver — 127 times, and started well over a thousand races in his career.

The President of the United States flew down to Daytona on Air Force One to witness his one-thousandth race.

They called Richard Petty, "the King."

And what a warm and friendly King he was! Richard's beaming smile, colorful outfits, and easygoing nature won millions of fans for the sport. He was never too busy for his fans and would often sign autographs for hours. Sometimes the line would snake all the way around the infield twice.

With his rivals the King wasn't always so friendly. He was a fierce and shrewd competitor, on and off the racetrack.

"Petty?" says Darrell Waltrip. "All I remember is that long finger in my chest and Petty warning me, 'Boy . . .'"

Tradin' Paint

The first time Richard Petty went around a race-track he wasn't in a race car . . .

He was *on* a race car.

Richard was thirteen years old. His father, Lee Petty, was one of the top drivers in the 1950s, when stock car racing was mostly small dirt tracks in small Southern towns.

Racing was a family affair in those days, and Richard and his brother, Maurice, helped in the pits, where the cars came in for gas and tire changes during a race.

During a very muddy race, Richard ran out with a rag to wipe the windshield while his dad's car was being quickly refueled. Richard was too short to reach both sides of the windshield, so he climbed up on the hood of the car.

Lee Petty wasn't a man to wait. As soon as there was enough gas in the car to finish the race, he roared back onto the track. He didn't see his son on the hood, trying to clean the mud off the far side of the windshield.

Richard held on as tightly as he could. He began to yell and bang on the windshield, as the powerful car slid around the corners. Lee Petty finally saw what was happening, but he wasn't about to lose his spot in the pack. So he kept going — all the way around the track at top speed, with his son on the hood, holding on for dear life!

Finally, Lee Petty swerved back into the pits and slowed just enough for Richard to slide off into the mud. Then he roared back onto the track and won the race.

"Was I scared?" Richard Petty said years later. "You bet I was scared. Not of falling or getting run over. I was scared of what my daddy would do to me after the race. But he just hollered some; he never ever hit me."

The Pettys were racing's royal family, the first family to see four generations on the track: first Lee, then Richard, then Kyle and then — for a brief moment before tragedy struck — Kyle's son Adam.

Lee was a hard-charging champion in the old days of dirt-track racing. He went on to make his mark on the superspeedways, too, winning several championships. He is in the record book as one of NASCAR's 50 Greatest Drivers.

Richard surpassed him to become the King, the most successful and most popular driver of all time. Kyle is still racing today, the head of his own Winston Cup team.

Richard Petty — "King" Richard — grew up with racing all around him. When he was a kid, Richard and his brother, Maurice, would imitate their father and race everything from wagons to bicycles in the small town of Level Cross, North Carolina.

Before Richard and Maurice were in their teens, their father had them working on engines and suspensions, learning the key components of race car science.

Lee Petty looks into an empty engine well with sons Maurice (left), then age twenty-five, and Richard (right), then age twenty-six.

Richard specialized in suspensions — shocks, springs, tires, and steering. His knowledge of what keeps a car clinging to the track would help him later when he became the world's most winning driver.

Maurice tried driving for a while, but went on to become an ace engine man. In fact, Maurice Petty has built more winning engines than any other mechanic — 263.

Quite a family!

Richard was working in the shop every day after school. He liked it, but he wanted to try driving. He finally got up the nerve to ask his father. "Come back when you're twenty-one," Lee growled.

That's exactly what Richard did. A few days after his twenty-first birthday, he reminded his father of what he hoped had been a promise.

"Take that one," said Lee, pointing to a beat-up Olds in a gloomy corner of the shop. Richard got Maurice and a few friends to help (racing is a team sport, after all) and took it to the track.

Did he win?

No way. In fact, it was almost a disaster.

"I drove that car every which way but straight," Richard later said. "There were cars all around, bumping me. I hit the wall and tore off both fenders."

Richard got so confused that he decided to follow the fastest car as far as he could, then pick another fast car and follow it. It was a crazy way to learn racing, but at least he finished the race.

Tradin' Paint

In fact, he finished sixth. Not too bad for a first race against Fireball Roberts, Curtis Turner, and other early NASCAR greats.

But Richard still had some work to do. He raced for over a year before he got his first win. He wrecked five cars in his first fifteen races.

"I learned by watching the other cars and trying to do what they could do," he says today. "Daddy saw me for the first time on my fifth race. He told me I was running too low on the track, but I had already figured that out. I learned something at every race."

When Richard was starting out, he often raced his father, who never cut any slack for him. In fact, once Lee Petty contested a race's results — and won. The trophy was taken from the winner, who happened to be his own son! Another time Lee wrecked Richard on the track and stole a first-place finish from him.

"He was like that," Richard says without a trace of bitterness.

Lee Petty was one of stock car racing's first professionals, able to own and race his own cars and still make enough money to raise a family.

He won the first Daytona 500 in 1959, driving an Oldsmobile, and went on to win three championships and forty-nine races in his career.

He lost a few, too. Richard and Maurice never forget the time they saw their father's car spin into the infield, splash into a lake — and sink!

They watched in horror. Then they saw Lee Petty

bob to the surface and start swimming as hard as he could, as if he were still in the race.

Lee Petty never did anything the slow way!

Meanwhile, Richard was beginning to win races. In his first big year, 1964, his sponsor was Chrysler. Their "hemi" engine, named after its dome-shaped combustion chamber, was so powerful that NASCAR banned it because it won too many races. The fans were getting bored.

Petty wanted to stay with Chrysler, so he went drag racing until NASCAR relented. He was glad to get back to the stock car track.

Richard's breakout year was 1967. He beat his famous father's record for most wins. At twenty-nine he was the top driver in the sport. That year he also did something no driver had ever done. He won ten races in a row.

NASCAR had a new champion.

A King.

Richard was a great driver by the time his father retired from racing.

Lee had a wreck. Maurice and Richard had seen a lot of wrecks, but this was one of the worst they had ever witnessed. The car went end over end, and all the sheet metal flew off — the doors, the fenders, the trunk, the hood. Lee was pulled out barely alive. He was in the hospital for months, while Maurice and Richard tried to keep the family racing business going.

Eventually Lee Petty recovered. He even drove a few more races. Then he gave it up. It wasn't that he had lost his nerve. "It just isn't fun anymore," he told the boys.

He hung around the shop until he discovered golf in 1976. Then he started taking more and more days off to spend time on the links. Gradually, Richard and Maurice realized their father had retired from racing for good.

"It's y'alls," he said one day, throwing down his wrenches and grabbing his clubs. "I'm outa here!"

Racing was always a family affair for the Pettys. Richard's son, Kyle, grew up on the track, just like his father and uncle had.

His best friends were other racing legacies — Earnhardts and Allisons. They would swoop their bikes down the steep-banked tracks when the cars weren't practicing. They all wanted to grow up and become race car drivers. Especially Kyle.

I'm next, he thought. If his father was King, didn't that make him Prince?

Meanwhile, Richard Petty was winning more and more races, traveling around the country. NASCAR was becoming increasingly popular. The dirt tracks were gone. Richard was winning at the new asphalt tracks like Talladega and Daytona.

"I grew up in a different era," said Richard, when asked to compare himself with his dad. "The tracks were getting bigger."

The new larger tracks were called superspeed- ways because the straightaways were long and the turns were steeply banked. Meanwhile the cars were getting faster and faster. They were passing 200 mph — and getting airborne.

Spoilers — wings in reverse — were added to keep the cars on the ground. Top speeds were cut back by placing restrictor plates, which limit engine horsepower, under the carburetors.

But even with these steps toward safety, there were still some pretty dramatic wrecks at Daytona. At 180 to 190 mph even a tiny nudge can lead to a major crash.

Once Richard and his main rival, David Pearson, traded paint on the last lap of a race at Daytona. They both spun into the infield. Pearson's engine was still running, just barely. He was able to limp over the finish line, flat tires and all, and take the checkered flag.

The King could only sit and watch, fuming. Asked what he was thinking, Petty said, "I wasn't exactly hollering, 'Hooray for me.'"

Maurice and his big brother Richard made a great team. Maurice had tried driving, and even won sixteen top tens in the 1960s. But his real genius was engine building. And Richard had the outgoing personality and the extravagant signature (penmanship was his favorite subject in school) that the fans loved.

Once the brothers argued and split up. The Petty team was fined after a win for an oversized engine. Maurice took the blame. Richard was furious because his image had been tarnished. The brothers went their separate ways, but reunuited a few short seasons later.

Tradin' Paint

*   *   *

The fans loved Richard Petty and he loved them back. "I always figured it was the fans that paid me," he said. "They were the ones who made racing great."

He racked up 200 wins in 1,184 starts.

Richard's retirement was one of the most dramatic events in racing. His last race was the 1992 Daytona 500. The King almost won the pole. Could his last race be his last comeback as well?

It was not to be. Toward the end of the race, the King traded paint with Michael Waltrip. Richard spun into the infield, and his car caught fire. The fans gasped, but luckily it was an oil fire, which is less dangerous than a gasoline fire.

Richard was okay. He climbed out of the car and gave the traditional thumbs up. His race car was totalled but his sense of humor was intact.

"I always wanted to go out in a blaze of glory," he said later that day. "But this wasn't exactly what I had in mind."

Today it is Kyle Petty who keeps the tradition alive. He followed his father's and grandfather's footsteps into racing, just as he had dreamed.

In fact, Kyle won the very first race he entered. He didn't wait until he was twenty-one, either. He was still in high school. His father met him in the winner's circle.

"You know how to win, son. Now all you got to do is learn how to drive."

Dad was right. It was six years before Kyle won an-

Kyle Petty, thinking about his performance (he placed thirtieth) at the Goody's 500 in 1996, which was dominated by then twenty-five-year-old Jeff Gordon.

Tradin' Paint

other race. With his first Winston Cup win in 1986, he became NASCAR's first third-generation winner. In 1992 he surpassed his famous dad by becoming the first Petty to win a million dollars in one season.

Kyle is every bit as colorful as his father, only in a different way, reflecting a different era. He loves rock and country music and could have had a career as a singer. He has long hair and liberal politics, unlike his conservative dad, who counted Ronald Reagan among his many pals. Instead of a snakeskin-trimmed cowboy hat, Kyle wears a ponytail and an earring.

He doesn't have his father's incredible record of success, but he is definitely a serious contender. Kyle Petty is one of the major players in Winston Cup racing year after year.

He is also known for his generosity. Every year he mounts his Harley-Davidson and leads a pack of other NASCAR drivers in a cross-country ride for charity.

It's the only time they are riding in a pack and not tradin' paint!

"When we talk about racing," Kyle once said proudly, "we don't just tell old stories. We're trying to figure out how to make new stories."

The new story was the fourth generation of Pettys — Kyle's son Adam.

Adam Petty was clean-cut, unlike his colorful granddad or rebel dad. But he was just as talented. Adam's first win was in a go-kart. He was offered either money or a trophy. He took the trophy, on the advice of his dad who told him, "At this point the memories are more important than the money."

Adam "retired" from the go-kart circuit at age thirteen, but he couldn't stay away from racing. In 1998 Adam became the youngest driver ever to win an ARCA (Automobile Racing Club of America) Late-Model race. The previous record had been held by his dad.

Soon he was running a full season in the Busch series, finishing third in the Rookie of the Year contest. He found time to run in just one Winston Cup race, making history by completing NASCAR's first four-generation driver chain. This came only a few days before his great-grandfather Lee's death at age eighty-six.

Then tragedy struck in March 2000, during practice at a New Hampshire speedway. Adam hit the wall on turn three and was killed instantly.

The next day his fellow drivers showed their grief and respect by leaving a space between the lead car and the pace car — the missing pole sitter's formation.

Today Kyle never races without remembering his son. Kyle and his wife, Pattie, have founded the Victory Junction Gang Camp in his memory. Established on land donated by Richard Petty, it is part of a network of Hole in the Wall camps for seriously ill children, founded by film star Paul Newman.

It is dedicated to the memory of the fourth generation of Pettys to love racing. And to the champion who might have been.

The Allison Family

Bobby Allison after winning the twenty-five-mile race at the Daytona Speedway in 1968.

The Allisons, E. J. and his wife, Kittie, loved auto racing. But they thought it was too dangerous for their boys.

Not one to take no for an answer, their son Bobby talked them into letting him drive at a Florida track. At that race, he broke several records. He went down in history as the first driver to roll a car twice in one race.

His parents were not impressed. Bobby was told to concentrate on high school. And that meant no more racing.

But when you have thirteen kids, it's hard to keep track of them all. The Allisons kept hearing the name Sam Lunderman, who was winning lots of races around the Miami, Florida, area in the late 1950s. Bobby was out of high school and on his own before E. J. and Kittie learned that "Sam Lunderman" and Bobby Allison were the same person.

Bobby and his little brother Donnie were racing fans from the time they raced tricycles. Bobby loved cars, but Donnie had his heart set on horse racing, until he gained too much weight to be a jockey.

Tradin' Paint

In 1959 Bobby and Donnie packed up their things and drove north to Alabama, where they could be near the stock car racing action. At first they were so broke that all they had to eat was a fifty-cent basket of peaches. When they won their first $135 prize, they thought they were rich!

They won more races and bought a place in Hueytown, Alabama, where their parents eventually settled, too. With their friend Red Farmer, another Florida transplant, they became known as the "Alabama Gang," one of the most feared and admired teams in racing.

They ran in every race they could find, traveling across the country, sometimes working all night to get a car in shape to race the next day. Often the members of the Alabama gang took first, second, and third place.

Once Bobby showed up for a race out west and was told, "What a coincidence. A guy named Bobby Allison won a stock car race in North Carolina yesterday."

"That was me," Bobby said.

By 1965 Bobby had won in every lower division and was ready to move into the ranks of Grand National (now known as Winston Cup) racing. Bobby was a fierce competitor. He had an aggressive take-no-prisoners driving style, and he always ran first-rate equipment. His motto was: "Whatever it takes."

Both brothers had reputations for settling things with their fists — especially Bobby. His tradin' paint duels with Richard Petty were famous, and the two often came to blows after a race.

"Petty was the top guy, and I was just coming on,"

Bobby said later. "He seemed to take the attitude that he shouldn't be challenged. But I go into every race with the intention of doing whatever it takes to win."

"Bobby was like a thorn in our side," remembers Maurice Petty.

But the King himself, Richard Petty, is almost affectionate, remembering Bobby Allison as "one of the fiercest competitors that the sport has ever seen. We had many a great battle."

Donnie Allison was best known on the superspeedways. He also raced Indy Cars and was named Rookie of the Year at the 1970 Indianapolis 500.

Donnie didn't race as much or as often as Bobby, hardly ever turning in a full season, yet he still managed to chalk up ten Winston Cup wins, which is more than many drivers get in a full career.

Allison also battled Allison, and several races saw the brothers scrambling for first place. Their mom, Kittie, refused to play favorites. She said that all she wanted was a dead heat between the two brothers.

"Mom," said Donnie, "that could never happen! I wouldn't let Bobby win, and I know he wouldn't let me win."

When they weren't battling *with* each other, the Allisons were battling *for* each other. At the 1979 Daytona 500, millions watched as Bobby Allison and Cale Yarborough slugged it out on national TV after Yarborough had wrecked Donnie's car.

"Cale went to beating on my knuckles with his nose," Bobby said. "That's my story and I'm sticking with it."

Donnie Allison in Victory Lane after winning the Permatex 300 in 1977.

*   *   *

In 1981, after a spectacular crash at Charlotte Motor Speedway, Donnie Allison was forced to retire from racing.

Bobby kept on. He was busy dueling Darrell Waltrip for the Winston Cup championship. They took it down to the wire three years in a row, with Bobby finally triumphing in 1983.

By this time, Bobby's son Davey was already making a name for himself in racing. Davey and his little brother, Clifford, had started early, racing bicycles with their pals on a backyard dirt track in Hueytown. They were so serious they even used flags to start and stop their races. Davey usually won. His purple BMX was legendary in the neighborhood.

Davey's parents told him he couldn't race cars unless he finished high school. Davey was determined. He went to summer school so he could finish early. High school diploma in hand, Davey jumped headlong into the world of racing.

His bike-racing friends became his pit crew. Uncle Donnie and Bobby called them the "Peach Fuzz Gang."

Davey started in a 1972 Chevy Nova borrowed from his uncle Donnie and placed fifth in his very first race. His career continued to pick up speed. He was the 1984 ARCA Rookie of the Year. By the late 1980s he was driving Winston Cup cars, often racing against his father. In 1987 Davey became the first Winston Cup rookie to win a race since 1981 and was named 1987 Winston Rookie of the Year. He was the hottest rookie since Dale Earnhardt — the first rookie ever to qualify on the front row of the Daytona 500.

Davey Allison celebrates in Victory Lane after winning the Daytona 500 in 1992.

In those days, Davey's dad was the man to beat. Bobby was one of the fastest drivers on the track. His spectacular accident at Talladega in 1987, when his car went airborne at 210 mph, prompted NASCAR to use restrictor plates under the carbs to cut top speeds.

Father and son often went head-to-head on the race track, much to the delight of their fans. The 1988 Daytona 500 saw the famous race's only one-two father-son finish. The fans loved it as Davey led his dad toward the finish line. Then Dad passed him to win. At fifty, Bobby was the oldest driver ever to win the race. And although he didn't know it, it was his last Daytona 500.

Tragedy had begun to stalk the Allisons.

First Donnie was injured and had to retire. Then a cut tire at Pocono Raceway in 1988 sent Bobby's Buick into the fence. He had to be cut out of the mangled car, and many thought he wouldn't survive.

Davey became the head of the family overnight. He had to approve the brain surgery that was his father's only hope at survival. Bobby lived, but his racing career was finished. After the accident, the great Bobby Allison's reflexes were never good enough to let him get behind the wheel again.

Then, in 1991, at the same track, Davey's car flipped eleven times after tradin' paint with his dad's old nemesis, Darrell Waltrip. Davey was badly injured, but six days later he was back in the car. He was so weak that his crew had to Velcro his hands to the wheel. But he knew he had to start the race to get the Winston Cup points, and he took the family motto,

Tradin' Paint

"Whatever it takes," to heart. He drove five laps before turning the car over to a relief driver. Although he didn't finish the race, Davey proved that the Alabama Gang was still the toughest.

But is there such a thing as being *too* tough? Perhaps. Davey was known for being a little overly aggressive. Sometimes he got involved in crashes that could have been avoided. His teammates and his crew worked to cool him down, and by 1993 he had matured enough to avoid one of the biggest pileups in NASCAR history — a fourteen-car crash at Daytona.

"A year ago it would have been me," Davey said at the time. "But I've grown up a lot."

He went on to win the Daytona 500 that year, proving that the race goes not only to the swift but also to the smart.

Meanwhile Davey's brother, Clifford, at twenty-seven, was just starting his racing career, following the proud Alabama Gang tradition.

Clifford started out as a bit of a playboy, but his dad, Bobby, had helped him settle down and get serious. At a Busch series practice in Michigan, Clifford was feeling very pleased with his car. As he sped around the track, he radioed Bobby back in the pits: "Dad, we're gonna get 'em!"

Those were his last words. Clifford spun out on turn four and was killed in the crash.

The Allisons were heartbroken. Especially Davey. But he did the only thing he knew how to. He kept driving, finishing fifth in the race that had killed his little brother.

The worst and final tragedy struck the next year. Davey Allison took a day off and flew his helicopter — his favorite toy — to Talladega, his favorite track. He wanted to watch a friend test a car. But a cross wind hit while he was landing. The helicopter crashed, and Davey lost his life.

Davey Allison's funeral was an outpouring of grief from all of racing. One hundred thousand fans and friends attended his memorial at the Talladega track.

Uncle Donnie drove his nephew's car around the track for one long last lap. Then Donnie and Bobby stood side by side, as always, but they knew that the glory days of the Alabama Gang had come to an end.

Bobby and Davey Allison were both chosen for the list of NASCAR's 50 Greatest Drivers. Quite an accomplishment for Davey, who drove for less than seven full seasons. With him as with Clifford, one can only wonder about what might have been.

"I still cry a lot," Bobby Allison said as he was being inducted into the International Motorsports Hall of Fame. "Davey and Clifford were quite different. Clifford was the one who always looked for the fun things, and he got killed working. Davey was the one who worked hard, and he got killed playing. That's the irony of life."

The Waltrip Brothers

Michael Waltrip, who carried Winston Cup racing's longest active nonwinning streak (462 starts), celebrates in Victory Lane after winning the Daytona 500 in 2001.

Darrell and Michael Waltrip are brothers, but they grew up in different worlds.

Darrell grew up as regular kid in a small Kentucky town, hunting, fishing, and riding his bike too fast. Michael had a totally different experience. He grew up in the shadow of one of stock car racing's greatest and most colorful stars — his own big brother, Darrell.

They called Darrell Waltrip, "Jaws." Partly because he drove like a shark swims, cutting through the pack, looking for slower cars to feed on. Mostly because he had a big mouth.

When he arrived on the Winston Cup scene, he said, "I'm Darrell Waltrip from Owensboro, Kentucky, and I'm here to replace Richard Petty."

People couldn't believe their ears. It was too brash, too bold. They booed. They laughed. Then after a while they cheered. Because this kid could drive! Whether you loved him or hated him, you had to watch out for him. If you saw him in the rearview mirror, pretty soon you were going to be looking at his back bumper.

Tradin' Paint

Darrell was always in the hunt, tradin' paint with the big guys — David Pearson, Cale Yarborough, Bobby Allison, and even Richard Petty, the King himself. Darrell was fearless and he was fast. He drove for car owner Junior Johnson, former bootlegger and driver, who was the most loved and respected man in racing.

In spite of his bluster and his swagger, Darrell's success surprised even himself. "I couldn't believe I was there," he later confessed. "It was like a private club. I'm sure they were all wondering: Where did this kid come from?"

Darrell came from a pretty little tobacco and bourbon town on the Ohio River. Owensboro, Kentucky, is known for its flowering dogwoods, the world's biggest sassafras tree, and the South's best barbecue.

People think of Kentucky as hilly, but it's awfully flat around Owensboro. The roads along the levees are long and straight — perfect for driving. Fast driving. Maybe that's why the area produces so many race car drivers — not only the Waltrips but the Green brothers and Jeremy Mayfield (and also, coincidentally, the author of this book).

Darrell's grandmother took him to the races. He loved the hot summer nights filled with the roar of engines and the smell of gasoline. And he loved the cheers of the crowd. *They're cheering for the drivers*, he noticed. *What if I were a driver? They would cheer for me!*

*   *   *

Then one day he was with his dad at a hardware store and saw a go-kart. He couldn't stay out of it. The store owner, sensing a sale, made Darrell's dad an offer he couldn't refuse. And just like that, one of the greatest careers in stock car racing was underway.

Darrell was not exactly a model student in high school. He got into his share of trouble. Nothing big, just cutting up and talking in class — and speeding tickets.

"Waltrip! Slow down! Shut up!" people would say.

Darrell listened. He slowed down and shut up. He was never rude to his elders (unless they were race car drivers!). But he was already dreaming of the future — when he would be paid to talk on television; when he would be paid to drive as fast as he could on the track. Those Owensboro boys can dream!

Darrell graduated from go-karts to stock cars and began running around the short tracks in western Kentucky, southern Indiana, and middle Tennessee. He married his high school sweetheart, Stevie. She understood his dreams.

With a loan from his father-in-law he bought his first car. The year was 1971 and the car cost $17,000. Today that would hardly buy an engine and a set of tires.

He ran on dirt tracks where the cars slid around on rooster tails of clay. He ran on asphalt and concrete that ate tires like they were potato chips. He learned the "beat and bang" of short tracks and the high-

Darrell Waltrip, with his wife Stevie seated in front of him, waves to the crowd before the start of the NASCAR Winston Cup Series goracing.com 500 in 2000.

speed draft of the superspeedways. He put it all together into a style distinctly his own. He discovered that he liked talking to reporters, and that they liked listening.

"In those days," Darrell admits now, "I couldn't keep my mouth shut." Like another controversial Kentucky athlete, Muhammad Ali, he was always good for a sound bite or a pithy quote.

The press beat a path to his door. Racing was changing. The good ol' boys who chewed Red Man and said "yup" and "nope" were no longer news. What the press (and the public) wanted was a colorful, controversial winner who was willing to say what was on his mind — and who had something on his mind to say.

Darrell fit the bill perfectly.

At first they called him Jaws. Then as he mellowed (only a little), he was nicknamed DW, which he preferred. They still call him DW today.

DW's career was a bridge from the old days to the new. In the beginning he was a nightmare vision in the rearview mirror of Cale Yarborough, David Pearson, and Richard Petty. Then one day he looked in his own rearview mirror and saw Dale Earnhardt (the Intimidator) and Jeff Gordon hot on his tail.

He and Earnhardt had many famous duels. DW disapproved of the Intimidator's aggressive style because it caused too many wrecks.

Although not as aggressive as Dale Earnhardt, DW was fearless. Almost. The scariest moment in racing for him was when he saw his brother, Michael, spin into the wall.

DW ran over and pulled him from the car.

In a career that lasted almost thirty years, DW won three Winston Cups, fifty-nine poles, and four races straight. He did all that by using the superb reflexes, skill, and daring that every great driver possesses.

But he brought something else to the sport.

Patience.

DW learned that if you hung back a little in the pack and went easy on the gas, you could sometimes win the race just by eliminating one pit stop.

It didn't always work, and sometimes it was close. Several times Waltrip coasted over the finish line, already out of gas. But his smooth and smart driving won him eighty-four races — more than any other driver of the modern (post-1972) era after NASCAR cut the number of races per year.

The great DW continued to drive until he was over fifty years old, and his retirement was gradual. He tried being an owner, but he seemed to be best driving other people's cars.

"When you're the owner," he said, "you are more cautious, maybe a little too cautious."

He once even drove for Earnhardt, replacing an injured rookie. DW didn't care. He knew who he was. Still does.

*   *   *

DW went on to TV and radio as a sports commentator. He now announces the races in which he was once favored to win.

"Once I was the whole show," he said. "Now I am part of the show."

He is third in wins overall, and first in the modern era. He is now in Owensboro's Hall of Fame along with film star Johnny Depp, who is not nearly as talkative and almost as good-looking.

Michael Waltrip was also born in Owensboro. Racing seemed like a natural thing, after Darrell. Michael started racing go-karts, and sure enough, he got the great insight that comes to every driver: *A guy could actually get paid for doing this?*

Michael called Darrell, who was already making a name for himself on the Winston Cup circuit, for advice on getting into racing.

Darrell was having fun. But he was also learning that there's more to driving than just going fast. You have to please your sponsors, please the public, please your crew chief, please your team, and put up with thousands of NASCAR rules and regulations.

"It's not worth it," he told his little brother. Maybe it was just one of those days. But he knew if Michael really wanted it, he wouldn't listen.

Darrell was right. Michael was determined to make it in racing. He found the encouragement he needed from an unlikely source — a competitor. Kyle Petty.

Mikey, as he was called, and Kyle became best

friends. Michael even lived with the Petty family in North Carolina. He listened and learned a lot from Richard Petty — the King himself — as well as from Lee and Kyle.

Michael began racing stock cars in 1981. He moved up to NASCAR in 1982 and won the Goody's Dash title in 1983, showing DW (and maybe himself) that he wasn't just imitating his big brother. He had his own destiny on the track!

As Michael proved himself on the track, DW became more encouraging. But Michael knew he had to make his own way.

He found rides (racing slang for, "jobs as a driver") and won praise for his consistency and professionalism. In the beginning he wasn't winning, but he was always running near the head of the pack. It was clearly only a matter of time.

After a stint with the Pettys, Michael drove his own Busch series cars. Then he got a call that changed his life. It was from Dale Earnhardt. He wanted Michael to drive for him.

"I couldn't believe it," Michael said. "A lot of guys think Dale is mean. But he's a sweetheart."

Triumph and tragedy came together for Michael Waltrip in February 2001.

He had gone the longest of any Winston Cup driver without a win — 462 starts. Then his first win came in NASCAR's biggest race, the Daytona 500. He entered Victory Lane all smiles.

He had seen the wreck, when Dale Earnhardt had hit the wall. No big deal. The Intimidator had survived a lot worse than that.

But where was Dale Jr., who had come in second? Michael looked down the track and saw Dale Jr. sprinting after an ambulance. A strange silence fell over Daytona.

Michael's hands were filled with flowers but his heart was filled with dread. Then the words came over the loudspeaker.

"We've lost Dale Earnhardt."

For Michael Waltrip, the greatest day in his life had become the saddest. His boss, mentor, and friend had been killed. Triumph and tragedy collided at Daytona, and tragedy won the day.

The Jarrett Family

Dale Jarrett at the Pennzoil 400 in 2000, where he placed seventeenth.

The last thing in the world Dale Jarrett wanted to be was a race car driver. That's what his daddy was.

Dale's father, Ned, was a two-time Winston Cup winner, and the roar of engines and the smell of gasoline were as familiar to Dale as the sound of tractors and the smell of cows to the son of a dairy farmer.

Dale was looking for something, well, less exciting.

Like golf.

Ned was one of the old-timers who helped stock car racing grow up from an outlaw pastime to a respectable sport. He got into racing as an owner and a mechanic. Then one day he got behind the wheel and started winning races.

Called "Gentleman Ned" for his easygoing ways, he dominated by driving cautiously. While his wild friends like Fireball Roberts and Junior Johnson were power-sliding around the turns, with all the fender-banging that the fans loved, Ned was preserving his car for a last-lap run for the checkered flag.

And it often worked. He had fifty wins to prove it.

*   *   *

Tradin' Paint

While Ned Jarrett was driving, stock car racing was changing. In 1956, eight out of ten NASCAR races were on dirt. By 1963, toward the end of Ned's career, more than half were on asphalt.

Ned didn't like the high speeds of the asphalt-covered superspeedways. He thought the cars were outrunning NASCAR's safety standards. He was proven right in the disastrous year of 1964, when Joe Weatherly and Fireball Roberts both were killed in wrecks that they might have survived with safer equipment. It was Ned Jarrett who pulled Roberts out of his burning car after the fiery wreck that changed NASCAR forever.

Ned went on to win one more championship, but he was ready to quit. He was the only driver to retire as defending national champion.

Dale's friend Junior Johnson retired in 1966. Junior went on to become a hugely successful race car owner, while Ned became famous as a radio and TV announcer, often heard on ESPN, CBS, and TNN.

His son Dale was nine when Ned retired.

Dale grew up at the racetrack. His playmates were kids with names like Davey Allison and Kyle Petty. While his friends dreamed of racing "just like Dad," Dale was more interested in other sports.

He excelled at them all. He was a star quarterback on the high school football team and a standout shortstop on the baseball team.

But golf was really his thing.

Dale started playing with a club his dad had shortened for him. He spent a good part of his teen years on the golf course, and it paid off. He was North Carolina High School District 7 Golfer of the Year two years in a row, in 1974 and 1975.

Dale's golf skills did not go unnoticed. He was offered a scholarship to the University of South Carolina, but turned it down to get married. With college on the back burner, Dale sort of drifted. He wasn't exactly sure what he wanted to do with his life.

He got a job at the Hickory Motor Speedway (where his dad was part owner), taking tickets, selling popcorn, and mowing the grass. Dale hated mowing so he bought some goats and turned them loose in the infield. That didn't work out too well. He had to get rid of them after they ate the dashboards and upholstery out of several cars!

On his lunch hour Dale would hit golf balls and daydream. He and his wife had a son, Jason, before divorcing. Then Dale met and married a pretty, young schoolteacher named Kelley. His life changed for the better, and he started to drive. Soon it was clear that Dale had inherited his dad's talent for the sport.

He won Rookie of the Year when he was twenty-one. In 1982, he moved up to the Busch series.

Unlike his dad, Dale Jarrett was comfortable with the high speeds of the superspeedways. He won his first Winston Cup race, the Champion 400 in Michigan, in 1991. But bad luck and breakdowns dogged him until 1993, when all the elements for victory came together at the big one — Daytona.

Tradin' Paint

*   *   *

After qualifying first and second, Dale Jarrett and his childhood friend Kyle Petty shared the front row at the start of the 1993 Daytona 500.

Kyle was knocked out of the race in a wreck. Dale was tradin' paint with front-runner Dale Earnhardt when he slipped past him on the last lap and pulled into the lead.

The TV announcer suddenly lost his cool.

"Come on, Dale. Go, baby, go!"

Very unprofessional. But the other announcers forgave their colleague, Ned Jarrett, when they saw the tears of pride in his eyes as his son took the checkered flag.

Ned's pride grew even greater a few years later when Dale won the 1999 Winston Cup championship. Ned and Dale were the second father-son champions, after Lee and Richard Petty.

By then, Dale's own son Jason was making a mark in the Busch series. Jason was named local Rookie of the Year seventeen years after his father won the same honor.

In 1998 Ned retired from announcing. But he still loves racing, and he likes to be introduced not as Ned Jarrett, NASCAR legend and popular TV personality, but as Dale Jarrett's dad and Jason Jarrett's grandfather.

"Those kids'll make me famous one of these days," Ned says with a twinkle in his eye.

The Labonte Brothers

Terry Labonte after his qualifying run for the Goody's 500 in 1999. He qualified for the ninth position.

Terry and Bobby Labonte were the first siblings to win Winston Cup championships.

Terry, the big brother, went first.

Although he has three different nicknames, (the Iceman, the Ironman, and Texas Terry), Terry Labonte is known for consistency. Like all NASCAR pros, he loves to win races. But unlike some, he understands the importance of finishing as many races as possible.

Terry Labonte hates to see a DNF (Did Not Finish) on his stats. And his consistency has paid off. He has two Winston Cup championships to prove it.

Born in Corpus Christi, Texas, in 1956, Terrence Lee Labonte fell in love at age seven . . . with a car.

He was a goner the first time he saw a quarter midget. It was a race car just for kids, with a fiberglass body and a one-cylinder air-cooled engine. Terry's dad, Bob, placed his son in the seat, put his hands on the wheel, his foot on the gas . . .

And Terry Labonte never looked back.

He started getting checkered flags right away. By the time his little brother, Bobby, was walking, Terry was already a champion. After winning regional and national championships, he moved into stock cars.

Racing a homebuilt '57 Chevy, Terry won his class at the local speedway. Then he moved up to Late Models, running both dirt and asphalt tracks in the same car — often working all night to change shocks, springs, tires, and gears for the next race. The whole family got involved, traveling in a motor home from track to track in San Antonio, Dallas, Fort Worth.

Meanwhile Bobby was racing quarter midgets . . . and watching . . . and learning.

In 1977 Terry found what every serious driver is looking for — a backer. Billy Hagan was a Texas oilman who fielded a Winston Cup team. Hagan told the young Texas champ that he would put him in the driver's seat — if he moved to North Carolina.

So Terry drove his Chevy pickup east. "I didn't have much," Terry remembers. "My mother made me take all my trophies, clothes, TV, and stereo. I had fifteen hundred dollars in cash. That was all."

The next year, at the ripe old age of twenty-one, Terry Labonte made his first Winston Cup start at Darlington.

In 1980 Terry barely lost the Rookie of the Year title to an up-and-comer named Dale Earnhardt. But he finished in the top ten in points. Meanwhile his brother and dad moved to North Carolina, too, and before long the whole family was racing.

In 1984 at age twenty-eight, Terry Labonte became the youngest Winston Cup champion of the modern era, driving a Chevy owned by Hagan. He did it in his usual calm, consistent fashion, with only two wins but twenty-four top-ten finishes in thirty races. It was a record that would stand until Jeff Gordon came along.

Terry left Hagan in 1986. A few lean years followed, but in 1994 he began driving for the fabled Hendrick team and his fortunes increased. In 1995 he became NASCAR's fifth "Ten Million Dollar Man," joining Bill Elliot, Darrell Waltrip, Rusty Wallace, and Dale Earnhardt.

The next year he broke Richard Petty's record of 513 consecutive Winston Cup starts, eventually going up to 655 before taking a two-race break.

Then in 1996 he and his brother, Bobby, won the same race.

Huh? How can two drivers win the same race?

We'll explain. But first, let's catch up with Bobby.

Bobby Labonte was born on May 8, 1964, about the time his seven-year-old brother was starting to race quarter midgets on the Texas tracks. Bobby started racing quarter midgets as a five-year-old in Corpus Christi. He switched to go-karts while Terry was driving stock cars, then moved to North Carolina and stock cars when his brother got his Winston Cup ride.

Bobby and his father, Bob, both went to work in Hagan's shop. But when Terry left Hagan in 1986, they both got fired — and struck out on their own.

Bobby started racing Late Models and won a championship at Caraway Speedway in North Carolina in 1987. He moved up to NASCAR Busch Series in 1990, with his dad as crew chief. He won a Busch series championship in 1991 and missed a second one by only three points in 1992. Bobby was clearly ready to move up to the Winston Cup. In 1993 he was runner-up for Rookie of the Year.

Meanwhile Terry was in a slump, going four seasons without a win. Then he signed with the Hendrick team in 1994. Hendrick Motorsports meant better cars, faster pit crews and, hopefully, more wins. Terry was pumped.

Bobby had also secured a faster ride — with owner Joe Gibbs, former head coach of the NFL Washington Redskins.

By 1995, both Labonte brothers were running at the head of the pack. In fact, they finished first and second in two races that year, with Terry right behind his little brother both times.

"This is getting old," Terry quipped. But he was clearly pleased at the way his career and that of his brother were improving.

And things were about to get even better for both Labontes.

In 1996 Terry Labonte and Jeff Gordon battled for the Winston Cup championship. Gordon was on a roll, having won the year before. Jeff won more races but Terry was more consistent, always finishing near the front of the pack. And it's consistency that wins the all-important Winston Cup points.

Bobby Labonte celebrates his fourth-place finish in the Pennzoil 400 in 2000.

Meanwhile Bobby was having only a so-so year, with no wins at all. Both brothers felt the pressure. "Our heads were in a vice because we hadn't won a race," Bobby remembers.

The Atlanta 500 started with Bobby on the pole and Terry qualifying third. Terry was driving with a broken left hand, but he knew that all he had to do was finish eighth or better and the Winston Cup was his.

Bobby took the checkered flag after a daring three-wide pass around Jeff Gordon and Chad Little. Terry came in fifth — but won the championship. Bobby had won the battle, and Terry had won the war!

In the end the two brothers drove the victory lap together, bathed in the cheers of fans, friends, and family.

Terry refers to that moment as "the most memorable time I've ever had in racing. Nothing else comes close."

Bobby's career high point came in 2000 when he won the Winston Cup championship for himself, putting the Labonte brothers in the history books once again.

The Earnhardt Family

The Intimidator enjoys a moment of relaxation at the Pennzoil 400 in 2000.

The Man in Black started out in a pink race car. Not on purpose. It was supposed to be purple but somebody mixed the paint wrong. Young Dale Earnhardt didn't care. He just wanted to get behind the wheel and drive. It was all he had ever wanted to do. He came from a racing family, and he spent his youth helping his father build winning race cars. His story really begins with his father, Ralph, who stands alongside his son in history as one of NASCAR's 50 Greatest Drivers.

And his father's story begins during the earliest days of stock car racing. . . .

It all started in the South in the 1940s. Bootleggers would smuggle illegal moonshine made in mountain stills into the big cities of Atlanta, Knoxville, and Charlotte. They souped up their cars to outrun the police.

The bootleggers were proud of their fast cars. Sometimes they would carve a track out of a pasture and race one another for fun. People came to watch, and one day somebody got the idea of charging admission. That was the beginning of stock car racing!

Ralph Earnhardt wasn't a bootlegger, but he was

one of the mechanics who souped up their cars. If you wanted a car that would outrun the cops, you went to Ralph's little shop on Sedan Avenue in Kannapolis, North Carolina. Dual exhaust pipes, shaved heads for more compression, extra carburetors — Ralph could do it all.

When stock car racing got popular and started awarding cash prizes, Ralph Earnhardt decided to try driving. He was as good behind the wheel as he was under the hood, and soon he was winning races at little dirt tracks all across the South.

Ralph taught his son Dale the tricks of intimidation. He would arrive early for a race, with his car ready to run. While the other drivers were tinkering, desperately making last-minute adjustments, Ralph would be leaning on a fender, staring into space, looking bored.

It was all an act, but it made the other drivers nervous, wondering why he was so confident. Dale, the man later known as "The Intimidator," watched his father closely and learned the lesson well.

Dale Earnhardt worshipped his dad. He wanted to be exactly like him. It was this desire that led to their worst falling out. Dale quit school in the ninth grade so he could work on cars full time. His father was furious.

"It was the only thing I let my daddy down over," Dale said later, with regret. "He wanted me to finish. It was the only thing he ever pleaded with me to do. But I was so hardheaded!"

Even though Dale became a multimillionaire, he always regretted the fact that he had dropped out of school, calling it "a fool thing to do."

Ralph Earnhardt had a stellar career in stock car racing. In the 1950s and 1960s he sometimes won four races a week. He won so many races at one track that he was banned because the fans quit coming!

Meanwhile, his son Dale was winning a few races, but losing many more. His father helped him out in the beginning, but left him to learn on his own. Ralph was big time. Dale was small time. Father and son rarely ended up in the same race.

But once they did. It was 1972, on a small North Carolina dirt track. Ralph Earnhardt was the leader, and he had almost lapped the field. He got on Dale's bumper, and pushed his son across the line into a third-place finish.

"That's something you remember for life," Dale said with a smile whenever he told that story. It was one of his favorites.

One year later, Ralph Earnhardt was rebuilding a carburetor in his garage when he died of a sudden heart attack at age forty-five. Dale was crushed. But he inherited his dad's two race cars, and that immediately moved him up a notch in the racing world.

He moved from dirt tracks to asphalt. Throughout the 1970s he struggled. He worked as a body man and a welder to get enough money to fix his cars. Money was so tight that once he worked straight through Christmas.

Meanwhile, he was married and divorced twice. He

Tradin' Paint

was, in his own words, "wild and crazy, young and dumb."

But not behind the wheel. Dale Earnhardt was already showing the skills that would make him the world's most popular and successful driver. By the end of the 1970s he had earned his first Winston Cup ride. He won his first race at age twenty-eight after only sixteen starts and was 1979's Rookie of the Year.

The fans loved him. The "cottonhead" from Kannapolis was one of them — a blue-collar, working-class kid with grit and determination. In 1980 he became the first driver to win a Winston Cup championship only one year after his Rookie of the Year award.

In the early 1980s NASCAR was dominated by the Allisons and Darrell Waltrip, who were in the process of taking over from Cale Yarborough, David Pearson, and Richard Petty. Earnhardt ran with them all. He became well known for his rough driving style, which infuriated some drivers, even his friends. Often, at the end of a race, every car on the track was streaked with Dale's paint.

Dale called it "just racin'." Waltrip disagreed.

"For the first time in racing, they've found a way to put the hood behind the wheel."

Dale Earnhardt had a winner's way with racing. He knew the tracks and he knew the cars. Once he rolled into the pits with the engine shut off.

"The crankshaft is broken," he said. "I don't think it hurt anything yet, so I shut it off."

The crew chief checked the car. The crank was broken. Dale had hit the kill switch just in time, before the engine destroyed itself. But how had he known? A broken crank makes very little noise — at first.

Dale just shrugged. He explained that his dad had sometimes made him drive barefoot so he could "feel" what the engine was doing.

Another time he passed a car and radioed the pits. "So-and-so's car is about to blow a piston. I smelled it when I went by."

The car blew on the next lap.

Like his dad, Dale had a feel for engines.

Earnhardt's career really took off after he teamed up with car owner Richard Childress in 1984. He had driven Fords for a while, but he was happiest with Chevies, and that's what Childress ran.

In 1987 he won a race at Charlotte Motor Speedway after being nudged into the infield grass. Most drivers would have spun out, but Dale stayed on the throttle and went on to take the checkered flag. His "pass in the grass" is one of the most famous moments in racing.

Dale won seven Winston Cup championships from 1980 to 1994, tying Richard Petty's record. Along the way he married his third wife, Teresa, the daughter of a race car driver. She helped him turn Dale Earnhardt Inc. into a multimillion dollar business.

By the end of the 1990s the Man in Black, as Earnhardt was sometimes called for his black #3 Chevy, was the richest man in racing. He flew around the country on a Learjet. Fans around the world knew him, and they either loved or hated him as he battled a whole new generation of drivers, led by a clean-cut, soft-spoken kid named Jeff Gordon.

There were lean years, too. A crash at Talladega in 1996 left Dale with a broken collarbone. In 1997 he went for a whole season without winning a race. And the biggest prize of NASCAR continued to elude him — the Daytona 500, the lead race of the year, often called the superbowl of stock car racing.

Then in 1998 he scored the big touchdown.

Dale Earnhardt had started the Daytona 500 nineteen times, but bad luck always rode with him. Once he had run out of fuel; another time he had blown a tire. Twice he had led the race only to lose last-moment duels to Sterling Marlin and Dale Jarrett.

It was different in 1998. The Intimidator ran near the front of the pack all the way. Jeff Gordon's engine failed. A drafting assist from Childress teammate Mike Skinner put Dale into the lead. Drafting is when cars run close together to cut air resistance. It's an important tactic on superspeedways like Daytona.

When Dale Earnhardt took the checkered flag, even his oldest and most bitter rivals cheered. He had broken a fifty-nine-race winless streak. Pit road was crowded with colorful uniforms. The crews from every team cheered him and touched his outstretched hand or his car as he went by.

Even usually unemotional Dale admitted that his eyes were filled with tears. After spinning his Chevy to cut a perfect 3 in the grass on his way to Victory

Lee Petty, number 42, nosed out Johnny Beauchamp, number 73, to win the Daytona 500 in 1959. The average speed for the race was an unbelievable 135.5 miles per hour.

The Petty family celebrates Kyle's Daytona 500 victory in 1979. Kyle's grandfather, Lee, is on the left; his father, Richard, is second from the right.

Bobby Allison and his wife, Judy, celebrate Bobby's victory at the Daytona 500 in 1978.

Donnie Allison in Victory Lane after winning the Winston 500 in 1971.

Davey Allison, number 28, just before crossing the finish line to win the Daytona 500 in 1992.

The Earnhardt Family

Dale Earnhardt and Dale Earnhardt Jr. celebrate after the elder Earnhardt won the International Race of Champions at the Daytona International Speedway in 2000.

Dale Earnhardt finished twentieth at the Pennzoil 400 in 2000.

Kerry Earnhardt finished first at the Pocono 200 in 2000—the first win of his career.

Dale Earnhardt Jr. takes a practice lap before the Winston Cup Dura-Lube 400 in 2001.

The Waltrip Family

Darrell Waltrip's pit crew gets to work on his car at the goracing.com 500 in 2000.

Michael Waltrip crosses the finish line to win the Daytona 500 in 2001. He did not yet know that Dale Earnhardt, his new boss and longtime friend, had died from injuries suffered in a last-lap wreck.

Darrell Waltrip (right) and brother Michael Waltrip wait to qualify for the NAPA Auto Parts 500 in 2000. Darrell qualified tenth and Michael qualified twenty-first.

Bobby Labonte helps a crew member push his car along pit road during the qualification round of the Pennzoil 400 in 2000.

Terry Labonte watches his son, Justin, practice at Lowe's Motor Speedway in 2000.

Terry Labonte crosses the finish line to win the Primestar 500 in 1999.

The Burton Family

Jeff Burton finished eleventh at the Pennzoil 400 in 2000.

Ward Burton finished thirty-ninth at the Pennzoil 400 in 2000.

Matt Kenseth, number 17, passes Kevin Harvick, number 2, during the MBNA.com 200 in 2000. Kenseth went on to win the race.

Kevin Harvick during a practice session for the Winston Cup Dura-Lube 400 in 2001.

Jeff Gordon celebrates with his wife, Brooke, after winning the Pennsylvania 500 in 1998.

Jeff Gordon finished seventh at the Pennzoil 400 in 2000.

Dale Jarrett at the Pennzoil 400 in 2000, where he placed seventeenth.

Steve Park leads a line of cars at the Global Crossing in 2000. He narrowly beat out Mark Martin for his first Winston Cup victory.

Crew members work on Mark Martin's car during his last pit stop in the Dura-Lube/Big Kmart 400 in 1999. Martin gained the lead after this pit stop, and later won the race.

Jeremy Mayfield crosses the finish line at the end of his qualifying run for the Texas 500 in 1998.

Kurt Busch finished nineteenth at the Pennzoil 400 in 2000.

Tony Stewart started in sixteenth position, and went on to win the MBNA Platinum 400 in 2000.

Lane, the ninth-grade dropout said, "I'm pretty good at writin', huh?"

Dale Earnhardt took his son Dale Jr. to a go-kart track when he was just eight or nine. Dale would stand on the track while his son maneuvered between him and the wall, getting closer and closer on each lap.

Dale Jr. could do it, but he didn't seem to share his dad's passion for racing. He didn't get interested in cars until he started hanging out with his half-brother, Kerry. The two decided to go racing.

Their sister, Kelly, joined them. "Can't girls race too?" she asked.

Yes, they can! And in the early 1990s there were three Earnhardt siblings on the track. All three showed promise. But Kelly lost interest, and Kerry only raced part time.

Dale Jr. became a champion. Starting late, he soon showed he had the Earnhardt grit and talent. He was a Busch series champion in his fifth year, scoring seven wins and sixteen top-ten finishes. Soon he was a Winston Cup regular.

Like Dale and Ralph, Dale Jr. and Dale have traded paint. But whereas Ralph pushed his son across the finish line, Dale caused Dale Jr. to spin out and sent him into the wall. The Intimidator wasn't about to let anybody pass. Not even Junior.

At the close of the century, the Man in Black was still a strong Winston Cup contender, winning his biggest bundle of prize money in 2000 — almost four million dollars!

Dale Earnhardt Jr. takes a moment to reflect on his thirteenth place finish at the Penzoil 400 in 2000.

*   *   *

The 2001 Daytona 500 welcomed Dale Earnhardt not only as a driver and former winner, but also as an owner. Dale Jr. and Michael Waltrip, the little brother of his famous rival, Darrell, were driving Earnhardt Inc. cars.

Although he was a master at it, Dale always claimed to hate restrictor plate racing. But he won ten times at Talladega, more than anyone else. It was said that he could "see" the airflow around the car, sensing it the way a fish senses currents.

There was a big wreck toward the end of the race, but Dale Earnhardt and his boys managed to avoid it. In the closing laps, the Intimidator was right behind Michael Waltrip, who was going for the win. Dale Jr. was solid for second.

The elder Earnhardt seemed to be holding back, using his third-place position to block any challenges for the lead. Then a slight rub from Rusty Wallace — the kind of tradin' paint Earnhardt had been involved in all his life — led to a spinout, a hit from the side, and a head-on crash into the wall.

It looked like the kind of crash the Intimidator had walked away from again and again. The kind that eats cars and spits out drivers.

It wasn't.

Michael Waltrip rolled into Victory Lane a winner. He and Dale Jr. had finished one-two. This was the greatest moment of his life. His first Winston Cup win was the world's biggest stock car race.

But where was Dale Jr.? And where was the boss,

the man with the moustache and the sly grin? The Intimidator.

Michael cut the press conference short. An uneasy silence hung over the vast stadium. Hundreds of thousands of fans had seen the ambulance rush Dale Earnhardt to the hospital.

Then came the words from which stock car racing may never recover.

"We've lost Dale Earnhardt."

Dale Jr. began the work of mourning, helping to comfort his mother and his brothers and sisters. But he also continued to prepare for the next race.

Like his dad, he is a pro.

"I'm sure he'd want us to keep going," Dale Jr. says. "And that's what we're going to do."

Dale Earnhardt won seven Winston Cup championships, tying King Petty for the record.

But the stats don't tell the story.

The story was in the slight, wiry frame; the sly smile, the glittering, narrow eyes. The relentless will to win.

Dale Earnhardt was a blue-collar guy who gave ordinary working men — and women — a winner to cheer for. And cry for. He was the real thing.

President George W. Bush said it best: "He was a down-to-earth, straighforward, plainspoken fella — who was a star."

Jeff Gordon

Jeff Gordon celebrates his victory at the Busch series' Miami 300 in 2000.

By the time Jeff Gordon ran his first Winston Cup race, he was already a fifteen-year racing veteran. That's because he was behind the wheel at age five!

Jeff grew up in Vallejo, California, where his stepfather, John Bickford, was a car parts manufacturer. Bickford knew how to build cars and how to race them. He also knew a future champ when he saw one — even if that champ was still just a kid!

Tiger Woods and Jeff Gordon are often compared because they both had fathers who were patient coaches. They both reached the top of their chosen sport in record time. And they both have movie star looks and style.

Jeff started out in quarter midgets. By the time he was eight years old, he was the quarter-midget national champion. He moved up to bigger go-karts, and he kept winning races. His brightly painted car with GORDY on the side was taking more and more checkered flags. Everybody else was racing for second place.

Soon Jeff was ready to move up to sprint cars. The problem was that in California a regular driver's license was required on the track, and Jeff was only thirteen years old.

So Bickford built his son a 650-hp sprint car and took him to Florida, where a license wasn't needed. It's quite a jump from a go-kart to a 135-mph sprint car, and Jeff spun out and hit the wall on his first start. Bickford groaned and fixed the car. He knew Jeff would catch on — and he did.

By the time he was old enough to compete legally in California, Jeff already had a hundred wins under his belt. Drivers twice his age were complaining to the officials. They thought maybe he was a midget, passing as a sixteen-year-old.

"It was time to move on," said Bickford. "Too many easy wins can make a driver cocky."

Jeff's stepfather moved the family to Indiana when Jeff was in high school. Bickford sacrificed his own manufacturing business so Jeff could move on to the next level in racing.

In Indiana, Jeff was eligible to compete in the sprint car circuit. And he was near the Indianapolis Speedway. The legendary "Brickyard" was so close that Jeff could almost hear the scream of the engines and the roar of the crowd.

Jeff's dream was to become an Indy car driver. His hero was Indianapolis 500 winner Rick Mears. The way to the Indy car ranks was through the midgets and sprint cars.

Jeff was a high school student by day and a sprint car driver by night. He raced legendary champion Steve Kinser, who beat Jeff regularly — but not by

Tradin' Paint

much. Once Jeff came in second and got the thrill of a lifetime when Kinser casually said, "Hey, kid, you're going to be a good one."

Kinser was right. With his stepfather's guidance and grooming, Jeff quickly drove his way into the top ranks, winning a midget national championship when he was nineteen and the Silver Crown title for sprint cars when he was twenty.

He was still hoping to win a spot on an Indy car team when his stepfather made a deal that was to change Jeff's life forever. Bickford arranged for ESPN to film Jeff at the famous Buck Baker stock car driving school, in return for free tuition.

After his first trip around the Rockingham, North Carolina track, Jeff called home excitedly. "Sell everything!" he said. "We're going stock car racing!"

Sprint cars are one-seaters, but stock cars can carry a passenger. When his parents came to visit him at the Buck Baker school, Jeff talked his mother into taking a ride. He wanted her to see first-hand what auto racing was like. She wasn't too crazy about it.

"Slow down!" she said.

"I'm trying, Mom!" Jeff replied, as he tore around the track. "This car won't go any slower!"

While learning the tricks of the trade from the legendary Buck Baker, Jeff caught the eye of a Busch series car owner who gave him his first official NASCAR ride. And with that, one of the most astonishing careers in stock car racing history was officially underway.

Jeff was the 1992 Busch series Rookie of the Year, though he finished toward the back of the pack as often as at the front. Losing was a new sensation for Jeff. But he didn't have to endure it for long.

The Atlanta motor speedway track is one of the fastest in the NASCAR circuit. Winston Cup owner Rick Hendrick noticed a driver in a Busch race driving an extremely "loose" car (which means the rear end tends to slide in the corners). Hendrick watched uneasily, waiting for the driver to lose control and wreck. But instead, he won the race.

"Who was that?" Hendrick asked.

"That Gordon kid," he was told.

"That Gordon kid" was hired by Hendrick and dropped straight into a Winston Cup car. Hendrick also hired Jeff's Busch series crew chief, Ray Evernham, who put together a team called the "Rainbow Warriors" because of their brightly colored uniforms. Racing is a team sport, and Jeff Gordon started with one of the best teams around.

Jeff's first Winston Cup race was Richard Petty's last. The two superstars met for the first, last, and only time, though it wasn't much of a shoot out. Petty had a DNF, and Jeff came in toward the back of the pack.

Jeff Gordon was never one to hang around with the slow crowd, though. By 1993, he was Winston Cup Rookie of the Year. In 1995 he won the championship, replacing Terry Labonte as the youngest Winston Cup winner of the modern era.

Tradin' Paint

With the help of his lightning-fast Rainbow Warriors pit crew, Jeff went on to win two other Winston Cup championships in the 1990s. He became the youngest winner of the Daytona 500, and the only stock car driver to win at Indianapolis two years in a row.

And he won something else, too.

The girl.

It takes looks, brains, and talent to win the Miss Winston title. Brooke Sealy had all three. Crowned Miss Winston for 1993, she was in Victory Lane to present NASCAR rookie Jeff Gordon with the trophy after his first win at Daytona.

Jeff was used to being the center of attention. And it's not like he'd never seen a pretty girl. So why did he blush down to his toes when Miss Winston handed him the trophy and kissed him on the cheek?

"He won the trophy," Brooke said later. "And he won something else, although he didn't know it until later. He had won my heart."

Although the legend is that Jeff and Brooke first met in Victory Lane, it's not true. A friend had been trying to fix them up for months, and they had been to lunch together, though not on a real date.

Now they had officially "met," but they still couldn't date. Miss Winston and the other NASCAR models are not allowed to socialize with the drivers. This is because most of the drivers are married, and NASCAR is careful to protect its image as a family-oriented organization.

So Jeff and Brooke kept their growing romance a secret, meeting for dinner dates and long walks out of the public eye. Jeff learned that Brooke was more than just a sweet Southern girl. She had graduated from the University of North Carolina with a degree in psychology, and she had a deep interest in religion and social issues. Brooke learned that the driver from California had a serious and a sensitive side.

During his secret courtship with Brooke, people began to wonder why Jeff never dated or hung out with the guys. But Jeff just smiled and kept his secret until Brooke's reign as Miss Winston was up. Then he did what he had been waiting to do all year.

He married her.

A lot of people who don't know his long history in racing think Jeff Gordon came out of nowhere. They think he was an overnight success, but John Bickford knows only too well the sacrifices the family made. "We slept in pickup trucks and made our own parts," he says, remembering the long nights on the sprint car circuit.

The misconception doesn't bother Jeff. "All my life I've been the young guy," Jeff says. "If people don't know that I've paid my dues, it doesn't matter to me."

Dale Earnhardt, the Intimidator himself, once complained that if "that kid" won the Winston Cup, they should celebrate with milk instead of champagne. When Jeff won, he taunted Earnhardt, his great rival, by toasting him with a champagne glass filled with (you guessed it!) milk.

Jeff's all-American good-guy image is not just an act. He and Brooke are active in many charitable causes. He won the True Value Man of the Year award in 1996 for his work with the Leukemia Society and the Jeff Gordon Foundation, which supports children and families in need of medical care.

Jeff's good looks and polished manners have made him attractive to sponsors and fans alike, although there are plenty of fans who love to hate him. After all, he's not a good ol' Southern boy. He has those Tom Cruise good looks. And worst of all, he wins!

"I guess he's too good for his own good," quips Darrell Waltrip, who is never at a loss for words.

Stock car racing fans need villains as well as heroes, and Gordon fills both roles. He gets boos as well as cheers everywhere he goes. Infield stands sell ABG (Anybody but Gordon) hats and T-shirts.

Does it bother Jeff?

"Not so much," he says. "I know it's nothing personal. It's part of the price of fame. Once I was riding in a car with Dale Earnhardt, and they were booing us both." Dale said, "'As long as they're making noise, it's okay.' That's how I feel."

Jeff also remembers watching a race with his mother when he was a boy, when the crowd was booing Steve Kinser.

"They boo him because he's the best," Jeff told his mother. "I hope they boo me like that someday."

After winning three Winston Cup titles, Jeff lost his crew chief, Ray Evernham, who went on to start his own Winston Cup team. The Rainbow Warriors were replaced by a new crew, led by Robbie Loomis.

Today, Jeff Gordon is no longer the Wonder Boy but an established superstar in the top ranks of Winston Cup racing. Jeff is a three-time champion, a modern-day racing icon, and one of NASCAR's most active drivers in charitable causes — and he is still younger than most rookies!

Mark Martin

Mark Martin in Victory Lane after winning the Dura Lube/
BigKmart 400 in 1999.

Mark Martin has been racing Winston Cup cars for over twenty years.

He hit the ground running. In his second year, 1982, he was barely edged out as Rookie of the Year by Geoff Bodine. But Winston Cup is a tough field — some say the toughest in the sports world — and it was 1989 before Mark won his first race, even though he had been runner-up six times.

The next year was a big one for the man from Arkansas. He came in second in points to none other than the Intimidator himself, Dale Earnhardt. That earned the genial Mr. Martin a reserved seat at the Top-Ten Table at the Winston Cup banquet at New York's Waldorf Astoria. He could be found there just about every year after, except for a few slumps. He still hasn't won a championship, but he has assured himself a place in the history books.

And along the way he has won a lot of races. In 1993 he tied Jeff Gordon and Earnhardt for the most consecutive wins — four.

"The first time you ever climb into a race car," he says, "it's not to win a championship. It's to win a race."

Mark often has a problem with the incredible

speeds of restrictor plate superspeedways. Sometimes it's impossible to avoid a pileup.

"At those tracks, you can go for ten races and not be in a wreck, and go for ten more and be in a wreck every time."

Talladega is the worst, according to Mark. "It's great for the fans, with the side-by-side racing and everybody bunched together. But it's scary and it's dangerous."

The shorter tracks present a different problem: "By the time your spotter tells you there's a wreck up ahead, you're already in it!" Mark says.

Wrecks are just part of the business, though. "If your typewriter shocked you," he said once to a group of reporters, "you would come right back to it — because that's what you do. We drivers are the same. I've never seen a race car driver who was semi-hurt who wouldn't race." His greatest fear is that he'll see his car out there racing and somebody else driving it!

Martin prefers winding road courses with both right and left turns, where he is consistently at the head of the pack.

"Driving road courses comes naturally to me. It's just like where I grew up in Arkansas. The roads were hilly and curvy. You drove as fast as you could and tried to stay out of the ditch. Well, that's road racing!"

Mark drives regularly in Busch series races, although he is cutting back and concentrating on winning a Winston Cup title, the honor that has eluded him so far.

"It's pretty neat to have finished in the top ten in

the Winston Cup standings for all those years," he says. "But we haven't won a championship either. That's what we're all here for, the championship."

Going for the Winston Cup championship means going for points. "The richest race, the poorest race, the biggest crowd, the smallest crowd — they all pay the same number of points. That makes every race just as important as every other race."

Sportsmanship means a lot to Mark Martin. His fans saw what he was made out of in 1997, when he could have bumped Ricky Rudd out of the way and beaten him. But he didn't.

The fans appreciated it. So did Rudd's crew.

Mark just shrugs, remembering. "That's not the way I race," he says. "It was his race to win, and I would have been stealing it. I race people the way I want to be raced."

Mark's sportsmanship, his athleticism, and his will to win have won him a place in the Arkansas Sports Hall of Fame.

"Being honored with people like Nolan Richardson is kind of humbling. It shows how far our sport has come, too."

Mark is appreciative of the talent on his racing team. "We have some really great young people working on my race car — very young and very good."

The feeling is mutual. Mark is considered an ideal driver to crew for because he doesn't just "beat and bang." He understands the machinery that is hurtling him around the track.

Tradin' Paint

"He knows exactly which corner of the car he wants to make a change on," said his crew chief. "If it's front or back. It's a pleasure working with Mark."

Mark has enjoyed many successes, but life hasn't always been easy. Tragedy struck off the track in 1998 when Mark lost his father, stepmother, and sister in a plane crash. But he gutted it out and made his next race, dedicating his efforts to his family. Jeff Gordon barely beat him out for the win. But the week after the plane crash, Martin took first place. In an emotional moment in Victory Lane, he brought tears to the eyes of thousands.

"I want to thank the race fans," he said. "I cried last week because I didn't get to dedicate a win to my dad and Shelley and Sarah. This one's for them."

Like many drivers today, Martin works out regularly. "Staying in shape is a way of life. The competition is too fierce in today's racing. Todays's drivers are a new generation. They're all athletic."

When he's not working out, Mark is thinking — or writing — about racing.

That's right, writing.

Martin is one of the few NASCAR drivers who can also pilot a word processor or typewriter with consummate skill.

He is the proud author of *NASCAR for Dummies.*

"But hey, it's not really for dummies, " he is careful to point out. "It's for new fans."

And these days, that's a lot of people!

The Burton Brothers

Ward Burton watches practice for the Pepsi 400 in 2000.

Ward likes the outdoors. Jeff is a basketball fan. Jeff likes country music. Ward likes rock.

Ward has a thick Southern accent. Jeff's Virginia accent is so faint you'd take him for one of those Yankees who are becoming so numerous in stock car racing these days.

Ward runs a Pontiac. Jeff, a Ford.

In other words, the Burton brothers are cut from two totally different pieces of cloth. The only thing that unites them is their love of speed.

Oddly enough it was Jeff, the younger brother (born in 1967), who got into racing first. Both boys were encouraged in motor sports by their dad, a Virginia businessman. They both raced go-karts, and they both won.

But they were born six years apart. Ward, the older (born in 1961), went away to military school and then to college. Meanwhile, his little brother Jeff went straight from go-karts to Late Models, with his dad's help.

After college Ward raced motorcycles for a while, which was all he could afford. His brother was a local sensation in Late Models. Ward visited the track one evening and got the bug. Soon he was in stock cars too, struggling to catch up with his younger brother. With that, the competition was on.

The Burton brothers' sibling rivalry led to a famous encounter in 1987, on the South Boston, Virginia, track.

Ward and Jeff were running second and third respectively and, of course, they were both after first. Jeff, though younger, was the more seasoned driver.

The trouble came when Jeff attempted to pass his brother on the inside. They traded paint, which knocked both cars into a spin — and out of the race.

No one was hurt — at least not until Ward, furious, grabbed his little brother by the neck and almost lifted him off the ground. He had forgotten that they were at the track and that thousands of friends, fans, and family were watching. Suddenly he remembered. He looked up and saw the crowd. Then he saw his father, stalking angrily across the infield toward his sons. Ward backed off.

"It wasn't good for the family and it wasn't good for the fans," he said later, in a model of understatement.

Both brothers went into the Busch series in 1990, but Jeff beat Ward for Rookie of the Year. Both are Winston Cup drivers now. In 1994 Jeff edged out his brother again for Winston Cup Rookie of the Year.

Ward got his first first place in Rockingham in 1995. He then began to struggle, averaging nine

Tradin' Paint

DNFs a year in the beginning of his career. His second Winston Cup victory came in 2000, at Darlington. The end of the season found him sitting at the Top-Ten Table at the annual Winston Cup banquet for the second year in a row.

It was even better in 2000 for Jeff, who finished third in points behind Bobby Labonte and Dale Earnhardt. It was his fourth consecutive year to finish in the top five.

Jeff still races in the Busch series, as does his teammate, Mark Martin.

"It's fun," he says. "And it gives me more experience. The engines have lower compression and the cars drive quite a bit different, but you learn things that you can apply to Winston Cup driving."

Though devoted to driving, both brothers make time for life off the track. Ward, who was the top shooter on the Hargrove Military Academy rifle team, is an avid outdoorsman. His interest in outdoors and conservation led to the establishment of the Ward Burton Wildlife Foundation, which helps purchase land in order to preserve animals' natural habitat.

When he is not running down race cars on the track or restoring his authentic Appalachian log cabin, Ward hangs out with his wife, Tabitha, and their children, Sarah and Jeb.

Jeff is more likely to be found indoors, watching Duke basketball with his wife, Kim, and his two cats, Madison and Patches.

*   *   *

Jeff Burton holds his trophy after winning the Busch series' Outback Steakhouse 200 in 2000.

Tradin' Paint

And what rules on the racetrack, brotherly love or sibling rivalry?

Both.

Ward says, "You drive to win. But you don't do something that's going to put yourself or your brother in jeopardy, because the cost of that's way too high."

Jeff says, "I work with Ward on the racetrack as if he were one of my teammates. You're extra-careful with your brother or your teammate. But you try your very best."

Jeremy Mayfield

Jeremy Mayfield talks with his crew before the start of the Pepsi 400 in 2000. He went on to finish thirteenth.

Some might say that Jeremy Mayfield's racing career began when he ran his mother off the track. He was thirteen, racing go-karts, and already a fierce competitor. Judy Mayfield was proud of her son, but she was not the kind of mom who watched from the sidelines.

She liked to race herself.

But when she traded paint with her boy on the last turn, one of them had to bite the wall.

That may sound like the portrait of a young Intimidator, which is what Jeremy is on the track. But he's also known as a guy who laughs a lot and enjoys just hanging out with his friends. He is also known for his smile.

And why not smile? He's no longer an up-and-coming driver. He's part of the elite, the Winston Cup ones to beat. Even though he has yet to win the coveted championship, he has joined NASCAR's exclusive Million Dollar Club, made up of drivers who have had a seven-figure season. More importantly, he has reached for and grabbed his dream.

"As long as I can remember, this is what I have

wanted to do," Jeremy says. "Whether I was sitting in a go-kart at some weekly track, or a Late Model, or whatever . . . everything I did was to get to Winston Cup racing. It is all I have ever wanted to do."

Jeremy Mayfield's career began at the age of thirteen when he started driving on go-kart tracks around Owensboro, Kentucky. Teetering on the line between the South and the Midwest, Owensboro is famous for two things: great barbecue and great drivers.

Jeremy had a powerful role model and source of inspiration, fellow Owensboro native Darrell Waltrip. Like Darrell, Jeremy squirmed his way through high school (though he got better grades). When he outgrew go-karts, he moved south to middle Tennessee, racing Late Model stocks and working as a fabricator, crew chief, and even sign painter in order to earn "seat time" as a driver.

What's the difference between a winning driver and a mediocre driver? Perhaps it's a tiny edge of aggressiveness, motor coordination, or athletic skill. Perhaps it's just luck. Whatever it is, Jeremy searched for it, and he found it when he was still a very young man.

He drove ARCA stocks and was Rookie of the Year in 1993, with eight top-five and ten top-ten finishes. He caught the eye of several car owners — which was exactly what he had intended.

"Hey, guys," he seemed to be saying. "Here I am!"

As his career progressed, Jeremy Mayfield began to run Winston Cup cars. As the 1998 season closed, the 6-foot, 165 pound Kentuckian proved he was a strong contender by coming in third in points — after Jeff Gordon and Dale Earnhardt.

"It really didn't hit me until I saw all these television cameras coming after me. Man, I looked behind me to see who they were after, because I wanted to get out of the way!"

It was Jeremy they were after.

His first great thrill had come earlier that same year. It was his first Winston Cup victory, at the Pocono Raceway. Jeremy stormed past his hero, Darrell Waltrip, to take the lead, then held off Jeff Gordon for the victory.

Darrell and Jeremy later embraced. Though the two are from the same town, they are almost a generation apart. The first time Jeremy actually talked to his hero was on a TNN call-in show.

"He was supportive!" says Jeremy. "When you hear Darrell Waltrip say he's handing over the torch to you, that's definitely a confidence booster."

Darrell has been as generous toward younger drivers as he was merciless toward his elders. Now Jeremy has joined Darrell in Owensboro's Hall of Fame, which also includes the father of bluegrass music, Bill Monroe. Sharing the spotlight with them are Owensboro's other stock car stars, the fabulous Green brothers, Mike, Ike, and Jeff.

It must be something in the water. Or the barbecue.

On his first Winston Cup team, Jeremy was junior to teammate Rusty Wallace. Another driver might have an attitude. Not Jeremy.

"The quality that I see in Jeremy is that he listens a lot," said Wallace. "Not only does he treat me with respect, but he wants to learn everything he can from me."

A winner needs more than a watchful eye and a humble attitude, though. Winning takes talent, teamwork, and luck. Mayfield has all three. He didn't have to wait as long as some for his first Winston Cup win, but still the wait was difficult. He told everyone he wasn't worried . . .

But he was.

"We needed to win and didn't know how to do it," he said.

Confidence is the supercharger that gives Winston Cup drivers their kick. Jeremy felt it coming on after his first win.

"It's a great feeling. It's the way I always felt when I was running short tracks, because I was winning races. When your confidence is up so high, it's like nothing can stop you."

Jeremy's great strength is that he listens. He learns from the older drivers, and finds that most of them are eager to share — even with a competitor.

"The first time I raced at Darlington, I spent a lot of time asking the veteran drivers how to get around the place. Darlington is different from most of the ovals we drive on. The egg shape is pretty tricky."

It was Darrell Waltrip who gave him the best advice: "Respect Darlington and she'll respect you."

Jeremy is a thinking man's driver. He even writes a column for CNN Motor Sports in which he discusses

Tradin' Paint

everything from team dynamics to track strategy. He's especially interested in the mysteries of super-speedway drafting.

"Cutting through the air doesn't always mean just having the best aero package, though that sure helps a lot. It means being able to line up with the right cars and draft with the right people. Half your time is spent trying to get to the front and half your time is spent trying to hold on."

Jeremy now lives in North Carolina, which is where all stock car drivers seem to go when they grow up. Even the ones from Owensboro.

There he enjoys the company of the men he battles on the track, blasting Metallica out of the speakers of his awesome Dodge Viper, and training for racing as an all-around sport.

Tony Stewart

Tony Stewart hoists his trophy in Victory Lane after winning the MBNA Platinum 400 in 2001.

Tony Stewart has done something very few race car drivers have done. He has run in the Indianapolis 500 and in a stock car race on the same day!

And he's done it more than once.

Tony was born in the Hoosier State, in Rushville on May 20, 1971. His racing career began a few years later, in 1979, when he and his dad went to a go-kart race in Westport, Indiana. A track filled with speeding go-karts tradin' paint can be as exciting as the Daytona 500 when you are eight years old. Tony liked what he saw.

A month later Indiana had a new go-kart team, with Nelson Stewart serving as owner, coach, and crew chief to his son.

"He never let me settle for second," says Tony. "He never pressured me to be the best race car driver in the world, but he did pressure me to be the best race car driver I could be. That's probably why you see so much fire in me today, because he always wanted me to be the best that I could be."

When Tony wasn't driving go-karts, he was at the

sprint tracks, studying the tactics of the grown-up racers and dreaming of the day he would join them. Like Jeff Gordon, his first dream was to be an Indy car driver.

"My father took me to a lot of races, and I think from the time I was at a race and actually knew what I was watching, I knew that was what I wanted to do."

Tony Stewart learned from what he saw. He won two national championships in go-karts before moving up to midgets and sprint cars. In 1995 he was USAC's first driver to win the series' top three divisions in one season. And Tony was just getting started!

In 1998 Tony began racing stock cars in the Busch series. But he didn't give up the open-wheelers. That was the year he made racing history by competing in the Indianapolis 500 and in a stock car race on the same day. After finishing at the fabled Brickyard, Tony flew to North Carolina for NASCAR's longest race, the Coca-Cola 600.

Tony did it again in 2001, using helicopters and a Learjet to make the transition from open-wheeler to Winston Cup car. He saw a lot of seat time that day, and in two totally different types of cars.

"The Indy car is half the weight of a stock car," he points out, "with front and rear wings and aerodynamics that plant the car on the track. When you go to a stock car, it is twice as heavy, with wider tires and much less down force. You have to be much more patient with a stock car, and not overdrive the car. It takes some time to learn how it reacts."

Tradin' Paint

Switching from an Indy car to a stock car takes a driver with lots of intelligence and raw talent. But Tony Stewart is modest. According to him, it's no big deal.

"It's kind of like a bicycle. Once you've been on one, you don't really forget how it works."

Tony is the only NASCAR rookie who has sat on the pole of the Indianapolis 500. And that's not the only record he holds. His NASCAR Rookie of the Year performance in 1999 was the first time a rookie has finished in the top five since 1966.

Speeding down the track is only part of the race car driver's job. The driver must also be able to understand what the car is telling him by how it handles. And then he needs to communicate that information to the team back in the pits.

Tony is the first to admit that he is still learning. "I know what I want the car to do," he says. "But sometimes I have no idea what the team needs to do to make it right."

Lower a spring? Put in a wedge? Reduce the air pressure in a tire? Stock cars are different creatures than open-wheelers. What works on one won't always work on the other. Tony Stewart is busy sorting it out in his head. He will often ask for a change in practice, just to see how it feels.

"More information for my data bank!"

Meanwhile Tony is learning how to be an owner as well as a driver. He has fielded his own sprint car team. Tony won't be driving, though, or giving orders as crew chief. The driver is a friend. Tony's going to hang back and let others make the decisions. His job?

"I'll be writing the checks and scraping the mud off the fenders."

Tony Stewart and Jeff Gordon, the two sprint track drivers from Indiana, had a famous run-in one night at NASCAR's famed Bristol Raceway, considered one of the toughest tracks in the Southeast.

Gordon knocked Stewart into a spin that cost him a fourth-place finish. Instead he finished twenty-fifth. Stewart paid Gordon back after the race was over. He rammed Gordon's car into the wall on pit road.

Both drivers later apologized to each other and to the fans. The wreck on the track was "just racin'." But Tony takes responsibility for letting his temper get the best of him. He admits, "I spun him out on pit lane, and that was wrong."

Being a Winston Cup driver is one thing. Being a Winston Cup champ is another. A Winston Cup champ needs to have confidence in his team. Tony has it.

"You can be the best driver in the world," says Tony, "but if you are worried about parts falling off your car, you'll never do well."

Tony's confidence has paid off. In 2000 he led in wins, though he didn't win the Winston Cup championship. He finished sixth in points.

To win the championship, with its complicated points system, you have to finish in the top five more often, or the top ten, or just finish. Bobby Labonte, Tony's teammate, came in first by finishing more races. To win, you have to finish. Tony had too many DNFs.

Tony is learning by doing, and also by paying attention to those who have already made the grade. His teammate Bobby Labonte is his main inspiration.

Tony Stewart works hard, but he takes time out to relax, too. He may be a rising NASCAR star, but in some ways he's still a kid at heart.

Lots of drivers go fishing or hang out with pals. Tony relaxes by playing video games (driving games, of course) or playing with a remote-control car.

One of the first things Tony Stewart noticed about being a Winston Cup driver is that when he's home in Indiana, people ask for autographs.

"That's cool," he says. "I like that."

Even though it cuts down on the time he gets to spend with friends and family.

His advice to young drivers: "Be realistic. Work your way up the ladder. Take your time, be patient, and work hard. Not everyone will be the next Jeff Gordon or Dale Earnhardt."

Or Tony Stewart.

Steve Park

Steve Park celebrates in Victory Lane after winning the Dura Lube 400 in 2001.

Steve Park was riding high in 1996.

The Long Island, New York, native was burning up the Northeast NASCAR Featherlite Modified series, on his way to winning a season-high fifteen wins across New England. He also won twenty-two poles and the Most Popular Driver award.

Steve had worked for years to get to this spot. He had gotten his start at the quarter-mile Riverhead Raceway on Long Island, where his father was a veteran and respected Modified competitor.

Steve had always wanted to race, and now he was a pro. He was right where he wanted to be. Or so he thought. Until he checked his answering machine. . . .

"I was living in Connecticut, racing about four nights a week, and pretty much on the go all the time. I came home one afternoon with just enough time to change clothes, check messages, and get a bite to eat before leaving that evening for another race.

"In the middle of all the messages came the voice of some guy saying he was Dale Earnhardt, and he was looking for a guy by the name of Steve Park. I kinda just laughed and continued on my way. I have a lot of friends who like to play a lot of jokes, so I figured that was just somebody messing with me.

"I didn't come home for about three days. There was another message from him. He wasn't as nice as he was the first time. I still kinda thought this was one of my friends playing a joke. But . . ."

But what if it wasn't?

Steve called his mother, a big Dale Earnhardt fan, and held the phone close to the machine so she could listen to the message.

"That's him!" she said. "I know his voice, and that's him!"

Nervously, Steve called the number Earnhardt had left. He got his team manager, Ty. "Hey, buddy, we've been trying to get a hold of you for a while!"

Steve almost passed out.

"Ty said Dale wanted to meet with me and asked if I could be at the airport at eight A.M. the next day so Dale could send his plane for me. I was like, 'You've got to be kidding.'"

But he wasn't.

Park was flown in Earnhardt's private jet from Connecticut to Kannapolis, North Carolina. He was given a personal tour of the shop by the Intimidator himself.

"That was really neat, because not many people got to see the real Dale Earnhardt. Dale told me the chemistry just wasn't there with his Busch team and that he wanted to make a change for the 1997 season. I thought, 'Why does he want me? I'm nothing special.' I guess you could say the rest is history."

Tradin' Paint

*   *   *

History is right.

Steve Park's next year with Earnhardt's Busch series team was a record breaker. Three wins, twelve top-fives, and twenty top-ten finishes.

The records fell like dominoes. It was the best season a Busch series rookie ever had. Steve Park took home over $700,000 in winnings. And he was named Rookie of the Year.

Earnhardt, never slow to spot a champ, bumped Park up to a Winston Cup car. Then bad luck struck like lightning: Steve was in a bad wreck while practicing at Atlanta Speedway. He had a broken leg and collarbone. The doctors said it would take him six months to recover.

Earnhardt surprised everyone again by hiring a racing legend, his ancient rival Darrell Waltrip, to replace Park.

Steve's next few years were dogged by bad luck and mistakes. A bad carburetor, the wrong tires, a spin on someone else's oil slick . . . the misfortunes just kept piling up.

Steve motored on, though, and finally, on August 13, 2000, bagged his first Winston Cup win in his home state of New York. It was the fabled Watkins Glen road race, the bane of many stock car drivers who think, "left turn only."

Steve's Winston Cup career reignited with the turn of the new century. He has placed in the top-ten in no fewer than thirteen races and has earned over two million dollars.

*   *   *

Steve now lives in North Carolina like so many other stock car drivers. He watches reruns of *Friends* and listens to Garth Brooks and other country stars when he's not working in the shop with the teammates he calls his friends.

Like so many others, he misses his friend and mentor Dale Earnhardt. He has only one regret.

"I have always prided myself on having a digital answering machine," Steve said. "But I couldn't save the message because of the computer chip. I'd love to have that answering machine message."

Kevin Harvick

Kevin Harvick celebrates after winning the Cracker Barrel 500 in 2001.

How many kids get a race car for a graduation present? Kevin Harvick did. The present was a go-kart, and the graduation was from kindergarten.

Kevin Harvick was born in Bakersfield, California, on December 8, 1975, when the country was just emerging from the Vietnam War and the top drivers in NASCAR were all from the South.

King Richard Petty, the Allisons, and Darrell Waltrip dominated the sport. Who would have thought, back then, that Californians like Kevin Harvick and Jeff Gordon would soon be helping to turn stock car racing from a regional sport to a national sensation?

Kevin is from a racing family. His dad was crew chief for a number of teams in California's magnificent, mountain-rimmed Central Valley. Kevin learned about cars early. He would spend time in the shop while his dad was working. Kevin would watch from his playpen.

As soon as his foot could reach the gas, he was driving a go-kart.

Tradin' Paint

Kevin's dad was no chauvinist. He bought Kevin's little sister a go-kart, too. But when Amber hit the concession stand and got a bloody nose on her first time around the track, she decided to take an early retirement from racing.

With Kevin, it was pedal to the metal from the moment the flag was dropped.

After winning seven national championships, Kevin climbed out of go-karts and into stock cars, driving a Late Model car built by his dad. He won NASCAR's Featherlite Rookie of the Year in 1995, then took a break from racing to attend Bakersfield Community College. College life was appealing. But something was missing.

"The time came for me to make a choice about my future," Kevin says. "I either had to focus on racing full-time, or decide on a new profession and begin training for it. I chose racing, and I've never looked back."

Kevin's mother, Jonell Harvick, supported her son's decision.

"You only live once," she told him. "Go for your dream."

Kevin's big break came when he was hired by Richard Childress, the same owner who backed the legendary Dale Earnhardt and his black #3.

Kevin raced for Childress in the Craftsman truck series and then moved up to the Busch Grand National. In his first full Busch season, Kevin finished third overall, clinching Rookie of the Year honors and tying Steve Park for the most wins ever by a rookie driver.

It was time to head South. Good-bye California, hello North Carolina!

"Being close to the shop and the guys was one of my goals," Kevin says. "I know it's an old cliche, but we're more than just teammates, we're all good friends."

Opponents can be friends, too. Rival racer Ron Hornaday is Kevin's good friend. Kevin and Ron like to shoot clay pigeons. They had a great teacher. Dale Earnhardt himself.

"Earnhardt loaned Ron and me a gun to get started," Kevin recalls. "He sent a Remington guy with it, so we wouldn't shoot our feet off."

Kevin has adapted to life in North Carolina, but he left his heart in California.

"Bakersfield, in my opinion, is the center of racing out West. There are a lot of Featherlite Southwest Tour and Winston West series teams headquartered there, and it was a great place for me to begin my racing career. If I were not driving in NASCAR today, my first choice would be to return home and race on the tracks in Bakersfield."

Plus there's the food. . . .

"There is one thing outside of racing and family that makes me anxious to return home, and that is the Mexican food, especially Mexican fast food. It is home cooking to me! A lot of the restaurants that they have in California do not exist in North Carolina."

Got that, y'all?

*   *   *

Tradin' Paint

Being a rookie is all about learning from your mistakes. Kevin still winces when he remembers trying to pass Terry Labonte during the Daytona 300.

Daytona is a superspeedway where cars run at near-200 mph speeds. Drafting is all-important. Cars often run single file, bumper to bumper, to cut down resistance.

Kevin pulled out to pass Terry, hoping to take the lead. But no one else got out of line, and a single car on the superspeedway will find itself falling back.

"I made a go-for there at the end, and the go didn't go," said Harvick.

Modesty is not just about manners. It's about winning.

Kevin's girlfriend, DeLana, moved from California to North Carolina with him.

"DeLana and I had a bet as to who had the most junk, and she won, hands down. It was me!"

The first thing on the agenda once they got settled in North Carolina was a wedding. Kevin and DeLana started making plans.

With Kevin's full racing schedule, plan making proved difficult. But DeLana is a driver herself. She understood the scheduling problems. Kevin was concentrating on his Busch series driving, hoping to follow up a Rookie-of-the-Year title with a championship. Facing a full calendar, the two planned a February wedding in Vegas.

Then tragedy struck.

*   *   *

Harvick was thrust into the national spotlight when he was chosen by team owner Richard Childress to replace Dale Earnhardt after the Intimidator was killed at Daytona in 2001.

When Dale Earnhardt passed away, Kevin was very upset. The legendary driver had been a mentor and a friend.

Harvick went to owner Richard Childress, who as Earnhardt's longtime friend was shattered, and said he would do whatever was necessary to help pull the team together. Childress took Kevin up on his offer and placed him in Dale Earnhardt's spot. With that, Kevin was thrust into a role that would make many drivers nervous.

Nervous? How about panicked!

"Nobody said life was easy," says Harvick. "It'll be tough but we're a tough team."

Kevin and DeLana thought of putting off the wedding, but Childress encouraged them to go ahead. The team needed something good to happen.

They went ahead with the wedding but postponed the honeymoon. A big Winston Cup race was coming up at Atlanta Speedway.

"I joked to DeLana that I was taking her to Atlanta for a honeymoon," Harvick says. "Little did I know I was going to give her the best wedding present ever!"

Harvick did at Atlanta what no other rookie had ever done. He won in his third Winston Cup start.

Not even Dale Earnhardt had done that!

Tradin' Paint

To make it even better, Kevin had beaten Jeff Gordon, Earnhardt's fiercest rival, in a .006-second photo finish. It was only on the cool-down lap that he realized what he had accomplished.

After the win, Harvick rushed home to watch the race on TV.

"I can't remember what happened in the last ten laps!" he told DeLana.

The newlyweds bought a motor home, so they could travel together during the long racing season. They often park their motor home right in the center of the track, which makes for some early mornings.

"The jet dryers start prepping the track for practice pretty early in the morning," Kevin groans. "That can come as quite a surprise at seven A.M.!"

There were other problems. Their dog, Back Up, was put in a kennel after he barked all night and ate the motor home's carpets.

Sorry, Back Up. But Kevin can't afford sleepless nights. Not when he's filling the seat of a NASCAR legend.

In his on-line diary for SportsLine.com, Kevin Harvick lists three major events that came close together:

Feb 18, 2001: I lost my hero and teammate, and the racing world lost its greatest driver ever.

Feb 28, 2001: I married the love of my life and my best friend DeLana.

March 11, 2001: I won my first NASCAR Winston Cup race at Atlanta Motor Speedway.

These three dates have changed my life forever . . .

Team owner Childress is pleased with Kevin's performance so far. He thinks Earnhardt would be, too.

"What Dale wanted when he retired was to get a driver in this car that could go out and win. We're getting what we wanted. I can just see Dale's moustache breaking out in that smile. He would be happy right now."

Matt Kenseth

Matt Kenseth celebrates in Victory Lane after winning the MNBA.com 200 in 2000.

According to Mark Martin, "If you wanted to start from scratch and create the ultimate race driver — Matt Kenseth would be the one. This sport is hungry for new talent, and he's got it."

Kenseth is a go-fast kind of guy. Even when he's not racing, he gets out on the track in a street car and goes 125 to 130 mph. Never on the highway, though.

"It's safer on the race track, where all the traffic is going one way, and all the drivers are pros," said Matt.

Matt's favorite track is Dover.

"That's where I ran my first Winston Cup race. It's a track I like. It's fast with a lot of banking."

Steep banking on the turns keeps the cars on the track and "in the groove."

Kenseth made his first Winston Cup start in 1998 and ran his first full Winston Cup season in 2001, winning Rookie of the Year over his good friend and rival, Dale Earnhardt Jr.

Matt knows that qualifying depends a lot on the time of day. "As it gets later, the sun goes down and the temperature drops. The air gets a little better and your engine's able to run better."

He likes to run at night.

"There is always a bit more excitement associated with night races. I guess it has something to do with the fact that most people recall the days when they went to their local tracks on a Saturday night. It brings back memories. It really is the same for me."

Matt's memories are mostly good ones.

Like so many others who have been successful in the world of stock car racing, he comes from a racing family. He was born March 10, 1972, in Cambridge, Wisconsin. His dad was a driver, and he let Matt help prepare his car before races.

Was that *let* or *made*? Depends on who you ask. But either way, it worked!

Matt started driving when he turned sixteen, and soon he was tearing up the local Columbus Speedway. At eighteen he graduated to Late Models, and soon picked up his first Busch series win in 1998 with a dramatic pass around race leader Tony Stewart.

He got married to his sweetheart, Katie, after a sensational 1999 Busch season, when he got two top-ten finishes after only ten starts. He was battling fellow rookie Dale Earnhardt Jr. for the Busch series championship, but he got edged out two years in a row.

In 2000 Matt was Winston Cup Rookie of the Year. Quite an accomplishment in a year when rookies all but dominated the sport.

"These ain't your daddy's rookies," says NASCAR veteran Sterling Marlin.

He's quite right.

Like rookies of the past, this new batch is talented and eager. They started training earlier, and they take racing more seriously than many of their elders did. They are also backed by professional teams with the best equipment.

"If you're as talented as Matt Kenseth, you don't have to drive junk," says Marlin, who is both mentor and teammate to Matt on the Roush Racing team.

Matt is one of those drivers who finds the restrictor plate tracks easy. With his usual modesty, he says it's because the superspeedways are "ninety-percent car and only ten-percent driver."

Midwesterner Kenseth sometimes feels out of place among all the Southerners in NASCAR. . . . But only a little. There are some phrases that sound the same when said with any accent, and one of them is: "Start your engines!"

Kurt Busch

Kurt Busch celebrates his Craftsman truck series Motorola 200 win in 2000.

Kurt Busch knows about luck. He comes from Lady Luck's hometown, Las Vegas. He was born there on August 4, 1978, just after his mom and dad moved to Nevada from Michigan.

But luck alone didn't get Kurt into his first ride. He had to pass a test to become a race car driver. Several of them, in fact.

The first test was in school.

Kurt's dad raced dwarfs — $\frac{5}{8}$-scale replicas of stock cars that go up to 80 mph. It was just for fun. When Kurt was thirteen he asked his dad if he could drive.

"You don't want to say no or maybe," Tom Busch remembers. "So I told Kurt that if his grades were good in school, he could race."

Kurt got all A's (well, maybe a couple of B's) and a seat in a race car.

Move over, Dad.

Kurt began driving at Pahrump Valley Speedway, a quarter-mile clay track laid out in the high desert. He began driving his dad's car, but he was so good that he got his own. Soon he found himself racing against his dad. The father-son team of Tom and Kurt Busch usually finished first and second.

"Kurt had ninety percent of the firsts," says Tom, when he eventually decided it was time to retire.

In 1995 Kurt was the Nevada Dwarf Car champion. In 1996 he was Legends Car National Rookie of the Year. He continued to move up in the ranks, still maintaining his rookie status. And while he was driving, he was holding down a job at the Las Vegas Water Company!

In 1998 Kurt got off to a fast start in NASCAR's touring series. He was the Southwest series Rookie of the Year. The next year he was the first driver to win four straight races in a NASCAR touring series and the youngest series champion.

Then it was time to take the next test.

The Roush Racing "Gong Show" is the most awesome open audition in auto racing.

Young drivers are selected from a stack of resumes to try out in real race cars. They drive in front of a panel of experienced pros, both drivers and crew.

First there are practice sessions where the driver must evaluate and request chassis changes for the fastest times. Next comes a twenty-lap "hot session" with every lap and every turn closely timed.

The driver who shows the most improvement in speed and is the best at calling the chassis adjustments will be considered for the Roush program's next open seat.

Kurt took the test — and got an A.

*   *   *

Kurt blazed through the Craftsman truck series in 2000 with four wins, four poles, and five runner-up finishes. He won Rookie of the Year but finished second in points overall, losing to Roush Racing teammate Greg Biffle. Along the way he led more miles (475) and completed more miles (4370.8 of 4443) than any Craftsman rookie ever.

That year he also drove in seven Winston Cup races. No big wins, but he finished them all, even after tradin' paint with Dale Earnhardt Jr.

After only one season in the truck series, Kurt became a Winston Cup driver at age twenty-two. He is one of the few drivers to go straight from the truck series to Winston Cup, bypassing the Busch series altogether.

And surely the only one named Busch!

Today, Kurt Busch is busy trying to pass the hardest test of all — the Winston Cup circuit.

"The aerodynamics are the biggest difference with the Winston Cup cars," he explains. "I need to figure out the feel of these cars and know what to ask to have changed, versus the trucks."

Learning is what it's all about, and Kurt is good at that. He knows that although he's come a long way, there is more work to do.

"For me and the other rookies, it's a matter of being consistent at every track we go to. That's what the veterans are doing and what rookies try to do, so we've got to work on that."

Greg Biffle

Greg Biffle stands near the first turn at the Texas Motor Speedway in 2000.

Greg Biffle was born two days before Christmas, 1969, in the shadow of America's most active volcano, Mount Saint Helens. When you're born in the midst of all that action and excitement, you have to make a *lot* of noise to get any attention at all.

Pretty good training for a NASCAR rookie!

Greg is the first driver in the Craftsman truck series to win a million dollars. That puts him in an exclusive NASCAR club along with Darrell Waltrip and Bill Elliot.

Not that Biffle is racing for the money. It's the roar of the crowd and the scream of the engines that gets this young track warrior's heart pounding.

Like many of today's hot new stock car drivers, Greg Biffle is an all-round athlete. In high school in Vancouver, Washington (a suburb of Portland, Oregon), he was twice the state wrestling champ. He was also an accomplished high jumper.

In track and field, it's all up to you. In auto racing, it's all about working together. Greg moved from one of the most individualistic sports into what is perhaps the most intense of all team sports, auto racing. To get there he first founded a business, J&R Racing, building race cars in the Pacific Northwest.

Then in 1994 he started racing Late Models at Portland Speedway. He won sixteen of the first twenty-six races he entered. He was also winning local championships and was recommended to Roush Racing by NASCAR Hall-of-Famer Benny Parsons — and Roush never had cause to regret giving the rookie a seat behind the wheel of a Craftsman truck.

In 1998 Greg Biffle tore up the Craftsman truck series as Rookie of the Year. He also tied the series record for consecutive pole positions, winning three in a row! Then in 2000 he won Roush Racing their first NASCAR championship in the Craftsman truck series.

That combination of skill and daring won him a ride in a Busch series car, where he plans to spend a year or two before his first full season in a Winston Cup car.

So far, so good. Greg was runner-up twice in his first seven Busch starts. And he got his first trip to Victory Lane after only eight starts!

Greg's ability to be a team player has helped him greatly. He blames his failures on himself and credits the entire team with his victories. Perhaps because of that generous (and effective!) philosophy, he's also a successful motivational speaker. His sponsors often invite him to speak in the hopes of firing up their employees.

Some drivers are left-turn-only, but Greg Biffle likes the challenge of road course racing.

"You have to concentrate on shifting and getting the truck turned," says Greg. "I really like racing on a road course."

Not only diverse, he's also a thoughtful driver. After a practice he likes to get out of his truck (or car) and walk around the track.

"Your train of thought is different than when you are just sitting in that seat while they make all the changes," says Greg.

Even though he's still a rookie, Greg Biffle knows that winning races and winning championships can be two different things.

"It's all about racing smarter," Greg says. "What happens is, you're going 170 to 190 miles per hour in a group of three and four, and it's the heat of the moment. You're not thinking about taking it easy. You want to get to the front and stay there."

But championships are about points.

"If we can target a top five in each race, and make that our goal, and not make the high-risk passes to get second or third or try to win the race by making some daring pass on the last lap, we'll be okay," Biffle says. "If we don't do stupid things like that, we'll get ourselves a championship. That's the big picture."

About the Author

Terry Bisson is an award-winning science fiction writer who grew up in Owensboro, Kentucky, the home of racing superstars Jeremy Mayfield, Darrell and Michael Waltrip, and the fabulous Green brothers, David, Mark, and Jeff.

Bisson, who now lives in New York City, is the author of many books for serious kids and playful adults.

Check Out These Other Action Titles!

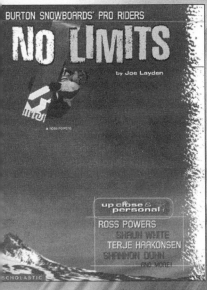

0-439-34277-5 • $5.99 US

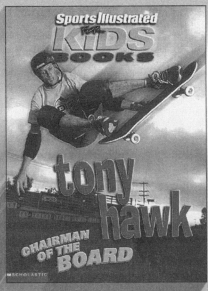

0-439-34293-7 • $4.99 US

A photo-packed insider's guide to the top riders in the coolest sport around.

World champion Tony Hawk consistently redefines the art of skateboarding. This is his story.

Available Wherever Books Are Sold.

www.scholastic.com

Other Scholastic Sports Books You May Enjoy

Michael Jordan
by Chip Lovitt

As a boy growing up in North Carolina, Michael Jordan dreamed of becoming a sports star. But he never could have imagined how successful he would one day become. Read all about the sports hero millions of people regard as a true American hero.

Mick Foley: Behind the Mankind Mask
by Terry West

This is the real life story of an athlete's climb from obscurity to superstardom — a story about a man driven to succeed at the one thing he loved more than anything, and all that he sacrificed along the way.

Tiger Woods: An American Master
by Nicholas Edwards

Tiger Woods has turned the world of professional golf upside down. But Tiger Woods wasn't born a superstar — that took years of hard work, dedication, discipline, and sheer love of the game. Here's the behind-the-scenes story on the making of a master.

The Vince Carter Story
by Doug Smith

Meet Vince Carter of the Toronto Raptors, a high-flying NBA All-Star. From his awesome gravity-defying dunks to his thrilling moves on the court, Carter has slammed his way into the hearts of NBA fans everywhere.

Yesterday's Heros
by John N. Smallwood, Jr.

Read all about the pioneers who fought for their place as African-Americans in the NBA — Earl Lloyd, Chuck Cooper, Nat "Sweetwater" Clifton, Bill Russell, Wilt Chamberlain, Dr. J, and more.